THE SPIDER:
THE PAIN EMPEROR

MASTER OF MEN!

THE PAIN EMPEROR

By Grant Stockbridge

ALTUS PRESS • 2019

CHAPTER 1
THE PAIN EMPEROR

THE CROUPIER called the winning number in an emotionless voice and Richard Wentworth's chips were raked in. He shrugged, rose with a smooth grace that spoke of perfect muscular coordination. "I'll be back, dear," he murmured.

Nita van Sloan's head tilted back so that he could look down into the violet depths of her eyes. "Don't be long, Dick," she said. Her soft lips were smiling, but not her eyes. They cried a warning. She knew that tonight, among these wealth-crowded halls, the Spider would stalk. And she knew, also that each time her Dick became even fleetingly that dread nemesis of the underworld, he took his life in his hands.

These were the thoughts that swarmed behind the veil of her violet eyes, behind the curving beauty of her smile. She said only: "Don't be long."

Wentworth's blue-gray gaze gave her assurance, and his glance about this room where danger lurked behind suave laughter was deceptively careless. Nita knew that the Spider would act tonight, but she did not know that he was walking open-eyed into a trap!

Tonight, Wentworth was trailing a man who called himself the Avenger. He was a mysterious underworld figure of amazing intelligence, and Wentworth recognized in him possibilities of

The mysterious poisonings, traceable to canned

great good—or diabolical evil. And he suspected that the evil dominated.

Somewhere among the excited groups of flushed, dry-lipped women and men with smiling lips and trembling hands, he knew the Avenger was waiting to strike, ready to spring his trap.

Wentworth did not know its exact nature, but he suspected that Stanislaus Mannley, the man who operated the gambling hall, was involved. It was like the first blind move in a unique

fish, meats, cosmetic, and cold remedies, were spreading into the thousands.

game of chess. A gambit was offered, and Wentworth willingly accepted it to learn the Avenger's motives.

Ordinarily he would have waited for events to reveal the Avenger, but time was pressing. The day's news had brought a hideous revelation. It was either a tragic accident or wanton murder. Forty-three men and women had been killed by poison in their food. It was a matter which the Spider hastened to investigate, alert as he always was to suppress the super-criminals whose attacks left police dumbfounded and helpless. For Wentworth, in his role as the Spider, had dedicated his life to the destruction of these fierce menaces to humanity.

Yet no man seeing Wentworth's nonchalant saunter would have suspected the thoughts that swirled through his brain, knowing that he was walking into a trap from which he might not emerge alive. There was a ready strength in the swing of his broad, perfectly tailored shoulders, a touch of arrogance in the poise of his well-shaped head.

He bowed his way past a group of acquaintances and stepped into the hall, furnished with the exotic luxury that Stanislaus Mannley everywhere affected. His steps were slightly quickened now, his eyes flashed alertly about. At frequent intervals along the walls, tall mirrors flanked by dull red lamps increased his range of vision, told him that he was not spied upon. He paused a moment beside a black Egyptian bowl, from whose depths rose the thin thread of incense smoke, a spiced and sultry scent. When he passed on again, a signet ring had vanished from his finger and a rosette of the *Légion d'Honneur* was gone from his lapel.

His fingers were deftly busy now. From a small kit strapped beneath his left arm, he slid out a black mask that would cover his entire face and a blond wig to conceal the crisp black of his hair. He need not hide the faultless black and white of his evening dress. Fifty other men here wore it tonight.

Before a door that was without label or plate he halted to

listen, then he thrust it wide and stepped inside. An automatic glinted dully in his right hand.

"I'll trouble you not to move, Mannley," he said.

A man sat alone behind a baize-covered table. He quit dealing cards for solitaire and said smoothly:

"Anything to oblige."

HIS JAW-HEAVY face was emotionless, without surprise, but there was a flare of light in his eyes. They flamed strangely with hate and that fact flashed a warning to Wentworth. Why should the man's eyes show hate? Surprise, fear, dismay; any of those might be expected, but not hate. Not hate, unless Mannley had been expecting him, the Spider. All criminals had ample reason to hate the Spider, who scourged their ranks ceaselessly, who slew without mercy to protect the nation and the people he loved from the forays of the underworld.

Yes, that flame of hate meant Mannley had been expecting the Spider, and that confirmed Wentworth's suspicions. This was a trap. His eyes hardened.

"You have," said Wentworth rapidly, "a check for three thousand dollars which was endorsed over to you by a boy named Shane Malone. I want it."

"You won't get it!" The gambler's heavy jaw thrust forward. He leaned slightly on the green-covered table and his slender, white fingers splayed out over the scattered cards. He was a corpulent man and there was a bulge in the breast of his stiff shirt.

"I see that you already know who I am," said the Spider softly, and he registered Mannley's start as one more proof of the trap.

"You know then that I am not averse to killing you. Will you surrender the check, or shall I take it from you… afterwards?"

Wentworth's eyes had whisked over the room, seeking the trigger of the trap. The place was empty except for chairs and this green-baize table, a liquor cellaret against the wall, a steel safe set into the wall. It was windowless, too, and the sole exit was the heavy door to Wentworth's left and slightly behind him. The room was sound-proof.

The gambler's hands pressed down on the cards until the finger tips spread in little balls.

"I'm not afraid of you," Mannley said hoarsely. "You're just a cheap crook, Spider. You pretend to be a sort of Galahad fighting crime. You go around killing people and printing that little red seal on their foreheads…."

Wentworth's left hand slid to his vest pocket and produced a platinum cigarette lighter. He thrust it out and touched its base upon a card that lay face up on the table. The card was the ace of spades and when he removed the lighter, a blood-red figure was sprawled across its black central pip, a figure that had crooked hairy legs and poisoned venomous fangs, the image of a spider.

"That was what you had reference to, I believe, Mannley," said Wentworth smoothly. Beneath the mask, his lips thinned into a smile to see the blood drain from Mannley's face.

The gambler licked his lips, began to talk more feverishly than before, spilling words that did not always make sense, heaping invective upon the Spider's head. Wentworth's lean, long jaw hardened. Small muscles bunched beneath his ears. The gambler was stalling for time. That meant the trap was to be

sprung through some one's interruption, that it was not yet time for the
intercession. He took a slow stride to
the edge of the table, the automatic
jutting from his fist.

"Quit stalling, Mannley," he said
sharply. "I swear to you that if you do
not give me young Malone's check within one minute, I shall
imprint my seal again, the next time upon your forehead beside
a bullet wound. I know this room is sound-proof. No one will
hear the shot."

With the muzzle of his automatic, he gestured toward a thin
expensive watch that lay on the green cloth.

"*One minute!*" he repeated.

MANNLEY'S EYES dropped to the platinum dial of the
watch, to the small golden hand ticking away imperturbably the
seconds of his life. He looked at the sinister red seal blotting
out the pip of the ace of spades. He glanced furtively toward the
door and the tip of his tongue touched his lips.

The Spider caught that side-glance and his eyes tightened. It
was from there the interruption would come—the blow of the
Avenger? But he must not show that he had seen the glance,
lest he betray his knowledge of the trap. His ear attuned to
catch the first whisper of sound, his eyes boring into Mannley,
he skimmed rapidly over the circumstances that had brought
him to the gambler's private room.

His ostensible purpose was to recover Shane Malone's check.
The boy had got over his head in gambling debts and forged that

7

check. It was being held over his head to force him to do certain criminal tasks—or such was the story that had brought him here. Wentworth's chauffeur, Jackson, who had been his top-sergeant in France, had given him the information. In a restaurant, Jackson had taken the part of a girl named Patsy Malone when she was imposed upon by her escort. She had babbled out the story of her brother, Shane, and the check, and Jackson had attempted to wrest the check from Mannley by force.

While Jackson was confronting the gambler, even as Wentworth was doing now, the Avenger had barged into the room and shot Jackson through the shoulder.

"Lay off Mannley, he's my meat," the Avenger had said, and then had fled.

It was a clever build-up. Those who were familiar with the Spider's crusades—and the newspapers gave him ample unwelcome publicity—would know it was precisely the sort of bait that would draw him. A young boy in difficulty with crooks, the Spider's own associate wounded. Yes, the Spider would hasten to make redress. But it was too perfect. And that was what had aroused Wentworth's suspicions, suspicions fully confirmed now.

The Avenger had publicized himself as a nemesis of the underworld, even as the Spider was. He had snared a number of criminals in a spectacular way, recovering thousands of dollars in loot. Other stolen property he had retained and spread broadcast over the city in the homes of the poor. Mostly they were gifts of money to the destitute that bore tags:

With the best wishes of the Avenger!

Newspapers had christened him the modern Robin Hood and Wentworth had been at first inclined to cheer him on—until the total of unrecovered loot had begun to reach enormous figures and he realized that large amounts of it must be sticking to the Avenger's fingers. Wentworth realized, too, what a threat to morality such a figure as the Avenger might become; how he might lead astray the youth of the land by his false example. And he had decided to investigate, to walk into this obvious trap and take the Avenger captive.

If the Avenger's answers indicated his efforts were honest, the Spider might even enter into a loose alliance for the suppression of crime. He bore no ill will against the man who was attempting to add the scalp of the Spider to his belt. But if, as he suspected, the Avenger's intents were to line his own pockets under the mantle of a bogus Robin Hood… Wentworth's nostrils thinned, his lips flattened against his teeth. Then, indeed, there would be a settlement.

BUT HE would need to be careful. When the Avenger struck, Wentworth must move swiftly and surely. The Avenger was a clever fighter, his scheme bore the imprint of genius, and Wentworth had no desire that his scalp should decorate the Avenger's belt. His eyes flicked to the watch. "Thirty seconds," he said flatly, "Thirty seconds to surrender the Malone check or die, Mannley."

"For God's sake," the gambler begged hoarsely. He lifted a perfectly manicured hand from the table and the fingers trembled. "Don't make me…."

"Fifteen seconds!"

"All right! All right!" The words stammered from Mannley's

lips. He moved the trembling hand toward his inside breast pocket. Suddenly his knees jerked upward. The top of the table bulged explosively and cards jumped. His left hand jerked into sight with a stubby, heavy-caliber revolver. It was a flashy, light-ning-fast draw, but it was suicidal.

The Spider's automatic barked and Mannley jerked spas-modically. His chair went over backwards and his feet flew high. The table leaped into the air and sprawled upside down on the floor. Cards sailed in all directions. There was no compassion in Wentworth's eyes. A crook had met his just end, that was all. In a stride, the Spider reached the gambler's side. His quick fingers withdrew the papers from Mannley's pockets, and there was a smile that was twisted into mockery upon his lips.

The Ace of Spades, with its Spider seal, had fallen upon the dead gambler's breast.

But the smile quickly faded, gave way to a frown. The papers he sought, the check of young Shane Malone was not in Mann-ley's pocket. Perhaps, then, in the safe… Abruptly, the Spider whirled, alert eyes on the door of this private room. His gun's muzzle moved with his eyes. His ears had given him warning.

Even as he spun, the door flung wide and a half dozen white and frightened faces crowded into the opening, a half-dozen witnesses that the Spider had slain a man!

CHAPTER 2
THE AVENGER STRIKES

C ROUCHED TENSELY, with the only exit blocked, the Spider nevertheless found time to wonder what had brought these people here. He knew that this room had been sound-proofed by the cautious gambler. It was here that he settled his crooked affairs, and he did not want the squeals of his victims—or perhaps a shot—to be heard by the innocents in his halls outside. Yet the Spider's shot had brought a rush of people. His lips thinned. Undoubtedly this had been planned by the Avenger. He hoped to trap the Spider without being himself exposed to danger.

The Spider's movements were a blur of speed. He reached the doorway in a long bounding stride, automatic blasting in his hand. His bullets, deliberately high, shattered the lintel above the opening. Hoarse cries of fright burst from men's throats. A woman screeched, throwing both white arms straight above her head. The Spider's shoulder thumped against the stiff white bosom of a man's formal shirt, slammed him against two other men and sprawled all three on the floor. Then he pivoted to the right, dived through a doorway to a window through whose pane the black iron tracery of a fire escape showed. He flung up the casement, then dived into a closet.

The door, shutting quietly, muted the excited shouts in the halls and the pounding of running feet. That would mean that all the gambling salon had been panic-stricken. All persons would be dashing for the doors. He hoped Nita would flee with

SHANE MALONE

PATSEY MALONE

them as he had instructed her to do if an alarm were given. He must remain, of course, for he had not yet achieved the purposes of his visit. He had barely escaped the Avenger's trap; be had not yet obtained Malone's check, nor had he met the Avenger.

Wentworth believed he ran small risk of identification by any one in that crowd that had stared in the door at the Spider, a man with blond hair and a black mask on his face. Yet it had been a comparatively feeble trap. The Avenger would not be satisfied with such a flimsy device. No,

MARTIN   COMMANDER SAMUELS

there was more to come. The Avenger must have been more subtle than that.

Wentworth thumbed out the nearly emptied bullet-clip of his automatic and replaced the cartridges. He carried another lighter gun beneath his right arm, but it was best to be fully prepared. The Avenger was no enemy to ignore.

He swept the blond wig and black mask from his head, dropped them to the floor. Over them, he spilled the contents of a small vial he pulled from the same useful kit beneath his arm. Then, listening a moment at the

BLANTON

JACKSON

PROFESSOR GOTTSTALK   THE AVENGER

13

door, he opened it and eased out. His signet was upon his finger, the rosette of an *officier* of the *Légion* on his lapel. He joined a group of men hurrying past the door.

There was nothing to connect this man with that nemesis of the underworld who killed in the night, the Spider. By now, the articles of his disguise had been eaten into a shapeless pulp by the acid he had poured upon them. A little while and nothing would remain but an evil smell. Nothing to connect him? Well, almost nothing. But the gun beneath Richard Wentworth's left arm would match the bullet that the Spider had sped into the gambler's body, if anyone should think to demand a test.

If Wentworth was worried over that possibility as he followed in the wake of the hurrying crowd, it did not show on his vital, keenly alert face. His mind was still busy with the fact that his pistol shot had been heard outside the sound-proof room. There was only one explanation; the Avenger had planted witnesses! A SLIGHT frown creased Wentworth's brow. This self-styled Avenger had sprung into being full-grown. One day, the man did not exist so far as the public knew; the next, his name was on everybody's lips. He had leaped into fame on the springboard of a famous kidnapping case. A prominent banker had been abducted, then freed when his ransom was paid. He had been unable to help police find his captors and the case had dragged along without new developments.

Then this man who dubbed himself the Avenger had called a morning newspaper and told the editor to go to a certain uptown apartment, and he would find the kidnapers, bound band and foot, with the ransom money beside them. And even as the

Avenger had promised, the kidnapers and loot were found. An hour afterward, the Avenger had called again.

A slight smile touched Wentworth's lips as he recalled the braggart phrasing of the Avenger's statement, as reported by the newspapers:

"I am a famous detective," the Avenger had said, "and I have ways of finding out what is happening in the underworld. From time to time, I will trap famous criminals and leave them for the police. I do not intend to act unless the case baffles all the authorities."

The Avenger operated differently than the Spider. He never killed. His prey were found always with the evidence of their crime beside them. In the month that had followed his initial effort, he had struck many times, snaring jewel thieves, payroll bandits, kidnapers, and once a murderer. He had promised next to turn up the slayer of a famous gang leader from Chicago, named O'Burke, whom police had sought vainly for several days. O'Burke had been shot down in New York.

Wentworth had watched the Avenger's progress through the newspapers—the Avenger reported every accomplishment directly to the press—and suspicion had begun to gnaw at his mind.

Then, on the day of the Avenger's biggest coup, these forty poisoning deaths had been reported, and, a day later, Wentworth's chauffeur, Jackson, had been shot. Wentworth had rushed to the hospital to find Jackson painfully wounded, but conscious and already out of danger.

"I'm sorry, Major," the loyal servant had said, calling Wentworth by his wartime title. "I'm damned sorry, but I ran afoul this Avenger fellow and he blew me down."

Jackson's story of championing Patsy Malone and attempting to recover her brother's check from Mannley still struck Wentworth as fantastic. Jackson, a squire of dames? It was incredible! Jackson was as hard-boiled as they came. A good man, but hard. And now, he became excited over a girl's misfortunes!

"What's she like, Jackson?" Wentworth had asked softly.

"Her name's Patsy Malone, Major," Jackson said. "Blue eyes, black hair curling around her face, about five feet two and peppery as tabasco. Why, she could have taken that bum to pieces if she hadn't been afraid of him, and…."

Wentworth smiled. "Okay, Jack, now go ahead with your story."

It was softly said but Jackson flushed. His jaw became stubborn. "Damn it, Major," he said roughly. "She's a square kid."

Wentworth made no answer and Jackson went on with his story. And so Wentworth had come to pay Mannley a visit, partly to avenge Jackson and help Patsy Malone, but more to meet this man who called himself the Avenger. There was small doubt in Wentworth's mind that the man was playing some deep game, and he was determined to fathom it.

WENTWORTH HAD separated from the panicky crowd fleeing from Mannley's. The gambling halls were nearly empty now and police had taken charge. A few men had remained, perhaps out of curiosity, or from sheer bravado. One of them might well be the Avenger. Surely the man would not give up without at least one more effort to snare the Spider.

Wentworth glanced about him, estimating those who had remained behind. Before this, he had found geniuses of crimes among his acquaintances. It was more than probable that the Avenger, also, came from that social stratum. He was too intelligent, his plans and their execution too clever for him to be classed as a common criminal. Wentworth had no description of the Avenger except that he was fully six feet tall and that his shoulders were as wide as a door.

He nodded greeting to a man who answered that inadequate description, Commander Samuels, a retired navy man recently returned from a business investigation in Russia. The man's round, jovial face, the light eyebrows like abbreviated hyphens, struck him abruptly as curiously mocking.

"Did you know Mannley had been shot?" Samuels asked, and in his voice, too was that quality of mockery.

Wentworth raised his brows. "Really?" he murmured. He strolled on toward the door of Mannley's private room, spotting on the way two more men who might fit such a description, one a croupier named Larue with a green eyeshade across his brows; another was a minor police official, evidently called from some formal entertainment. The official, striding from Mannley's room, stared hostilely at Wentworth.

Wentworth swept an exaggerated bow. "Deputy Marshant," he said.

The man grunted and strode on. Wentworth nodded to the patrolman at the door, showing the police courtesy-badge he carried and stepped inside. An officer he knew, Inspector Trowbridge, stood staring grimly down at Mannley's corpse, but they were the room's only occupants.

Trowbridge glanced up, his over-sized head bobbing in greeting on his stringy neck. "A nice mess," he said, thin-voiced. "A helluva nice…" He broke off, staring past Wentworth.

A sudden blow between the shoulders sent Wentworth reeling forward. He heard the patrolman's startled cry choke off, heard his body slam down and a voice ring out from the doorway: "Hands up, everyone! The Avenger is speaking!"

Wentworth whirled, but his hands stayed clear of his guns. The man who called himself the Avenger had shut the sound-proof door and his shoulders matched its width. He was dressed in black from head to foot, black dress suit, a black priest's vest over his shirt, a black mask that was a hood tucked inside a black collar.

"Here's another crook for you, Inspector," boomed the Avenger's deep voice. "This Wentworth is the Spider. You'll find that bullet from gun under his arm will match bullet from gambler's body."

CHAPTER 3
A NEW HORROR

THE AVENGER'S words sent a thrill of alarm through Wentworth's body. He had been conscious of the danger of that tell-tale gun beneath his arm, but he had thought it a minor risk. After all, how could anyone know that he still carried the murder gun? A tight wariness stiffened his muscles. Truly, the Avenger had planned well. It flashed through his mind that the Hooded One had prepared for all of this, even to the death of Mannley!

None of his swift fears, his mounting tension showed in Wentworth's face. There was mild mockery upon his whimsical lips and in his tip-tilted eyebrows. He bowed, clicking his heels. "Ah, the Avenger!" he murmured. "But you flatter me, sir, comparing my work with that of the Spider."

Through the drumming of his blood that was the tocsin of danger, Wentworth studied the man. He was attuned to peril and even when death gibbered at him his active brain reached ahead to the next move in the lethal chess that he played. He was seeking, even while he struggled for a way out of his dilemma, to find some characteristic to identify the Avenger. There was nothing except the man's size.

The Avenger was fully six feet in height, though the breadth of his shoulders made him seem somewhat shorter. His voice was thick with a suspicion of accent and he had the Russian trick of dropping articles before nouns. Commander Samuels might have acquired such a mannerism on his frequent expeditions to Russia. At the same time, either the deputy, Marshant, or the croupier, Larue, might assume such an accent.

But this was no time for speculation. He must worm his way out of this ingenious trap. The Avenger did not kill, but he might just as well loose the full contents of that ready automatic into his heart, as turn him over to police with the gun that could be identified both as his own and as the murder weapon. But there was no way out. The Devil! Was the Spider, for all his vaunted cleverness, to fall prey to this hooded Avenger in their first encounter? He heard impatience in the Avenger's voice.

"Come, come, Inspector Trowbridge," the hooded man snapped. "Handcuff Wentworth. You can get gun later."

Wentworth slipped out his cigarette case with fingers that did not tremble despite his tension. He tucked a smoke between his lips, snapped flame to it. His motions were sure and unhurried. Thoughts and abortive plans of escape darted about in his brain like imprisoned birds, but they all seemed useless. It would not do merely to attack the Avenger and flee, even if he could escape the menace of that leveled Colt's forty-five that was twin to the murder gun beneath his arm. To flee would be to confirm the accusation the Avenger had made. And Richard Wentworth, Park Avenue clubman, would become a fugitive from the law, his effectiveness against crime and criminals perhaps fatally impaired. Should he struggle with the Avenger, and in the confusion, toss the damning gun down the hall? He would still have a weapon, the lighter automatic beneath his right arm. No, that wouldn't do. Even if the murder gun were not found after he hurled it away, the empty holster under his left arm would accuse him.

A sense of panic strange to Wentworth shook him inwardly. Was there no way out then? Surely, this brain, these perfectly trained muscles on which he had so often and securely depended, would not fail him now! A pulse throbbed in the thin knife-scar upon his right temple. His whole body was tense with the need for action. He fought down his despair, made his voice cool and politely mocking.

"What are you waiting for, Inspector?" he asked. "Don't you hear the Avenger's orders?" Could he goad Trowbridge into open battle with the Avenger? It might help, though nothing short of Trowbridge's death could prevent a check-up of the gun. And Wentworth desired no officer's death, even if his own life hung in the balance.

Inspector Trowbridge had been standing, rigid with anger. Now his voice cracked in a curse. "Put down that gun!" he yelled at the Avenger. He thrust out his oversize head, leaned his angular body forward as he started across the floor. The Avenger's automatic swiveled toward him.

"Please to stand still," the Avenger barked. "I do not want to shoot you!" There was a flat menace in his voice that brought Trowbridge to a halt, his whole lanky body vibrant with anger.

"That's better," the Avenger said, *"Now put the cuffs on Wentworth!"*

WENTWORTH REALIZED that only seconds had passed since the Avenger had forced his way into the room, seconds that had dragged out hours long. Either Trowbridge or the Avenger would be forced to act soon, but he still could not see how either could assist him. That damnable murder gun seemed to burn beneath his arm like white hot iron. Its twin stared at him with a black, death-greedy muzzle. The twin....

The Spider tilted back his head to cover a sudden gleam in his eyes. He wafted a smoke ring toward the ceiling.

"By all means, Inspector," he drawled. "Put the cuffs on me. The Avenger has the upper hand and it will do no harm to humor him."

The inspector twisted his stringy neck and looked at Wentworth's smiling face, glowered back to the Avenger as if estimating the risks. The Hooded Man was no more than six feet away, but a charge in the face of that leveled automatic would be sheer suicide. Wentworth held his breath. He didn't want Trowbridge to attack the Avenger, not now. The Avenger must think he was winning....

Wentworth held his breath. He dared not urge Trowbridge too much.

Inspector Trowbridge grumbled, cursed and fished out handcuffs from beneath his coat. As the official turned toward him, Wentworth blew out his breath softly and tossed the cigarette aside. He put his wrists together close to his belly.

Inspector Trowbridge angled toward him, followed by the Avenger's watchful gun. The policeman on the floor moaned softly and the Avenger drew back his foot and kicked the man behind the ear without once taking his eyes off Wentworth and the inspector. Trowbridge was quite close now, reaching

Richard Wentworth

out the cuffs for Wentworth's wrists. As his bony, thick-veined hands came out, Wentworth pivoted lightly on his left toe and slammed home his right fist in an upper cut. It cracked against the Inspector's chin and sent him reeling backward with arms windmilling, reeling straight toward the Avenger!

Wentworth went in fast behind Trowbridge, thrusting him

violently backward with both hands planted on his flat chest. The Avenger barked out a sharp warning, but as Wentworth had expected, he did not fire. He could not afford to have the wounding of a police inspector set against his name to dim the Robin Hood legend he was building. No such scruples would apply to firing on Wentworth, of course, especially when there was a murder gun in his holster that would identify him as the Spider!

The Avenger tried to spring aside, but the inspector was already upon him. The two men slammed against the wall and Wentworth leaped clear and struck with both fists, knocking aside the leveled automatic in the Avenger's hand, cracking a right into the hooded face. The blow was awkward, half blocked by the inspector's body, but the Avenger's shot went wild.

He fought frantically to free himself of the half-conscious inspector. He slashed with his automatic, but Wentworth danced out of range. His fist snaked through again, thudded against the hooded face. The Avenger's arms jerked upward for protection and the Spider struck twice with all his strength at the nerve center of the pistol arm.

The Avenger struggled clear of his entanglement with the inspector, but his automatic dropped from paralyzed fingers. Wentworth sprang backward, snatching for his own weapon. He did a strange thing then. Instead of snapping his colt's forty-five—the murder gun—instantly from its holster as he knew so well how to do, he fumbled and barely got it clear in time to strike awkwardly as the Avenger closed in. The clubbing gun was seized in an iron grip and twisted out of his hand.

Wentworth dropped to one knee. His left hand flashed to

the lighter gun beneath his right arm and pumped three swift shots upward past his assailant's face. The Avenger spun about with a hoarse, startled cry and plunged out into the hall. Wentworth was after him in a trice, but brought up short as be heard the heavy boom of revolvers smash out. The hall was empty. Commander Samuels, Deputy Marshant, everyone had disappeared.

INSPECTOR TROWBRIDGE struggled to his feet, stood staring vacantly about. He realized the Avenger was gone and sprang to the door, but the crash of shooting had already dwindled, the chase had left the floor and rushed noisily on. Trowbridge turned slowly about, his big head, dark gray hair awry, thrust forward. He stared at Wentworth and his eyes got hard and round.

Wentworth laughed and threw up both hands, palms outward.

"Now, inspector," he said. "I apologize. I only hit you because there was no other way of getting at the Avenger." He dropped his hands and offered a smiling jaw for the police officer's fist. "Go on, hit me," he urged. "I deserve it."

The hardness went out of the police inspector's eyes and they became speculative, suspicious.

"All right," he said slowly, "but pull your punches another time."

Wentworth nodded and, with that suspicious gaze still upon him, stooped to pick up the Avenger's gun—the twin of the murder weapon—which he had wrestled from the man's hand. He tendered it to the police officer.

"Here's my gun," he said. "You'd better check it just to make sure the Avenger was lying. This is the only forty-five I carry, and Mannley apparently was killed with a forty-five. My left hand gun—" he displayed it on his palm, "is a thirty-eight. You know I have permits for a half dozen various guns."

The inspector nodded sourly, accepted the heavier automatic, but still watched Wentworth. However he gave grumpy permission for him to leave. He knew Wentworth by name because of his frequent visits to headquarters to visit his friend, Police Commissioner Stanley Kirkpatrick. Once out of the inspector's sight, Wentworth moved swiftly. In the gambler's quarters, he had spotted the safe which probably contained young Malone's note, but he knew that for hours it would be impossible to search it successfully. Meantime, there was other work for the Spider.

He had succeeded in routing the Avenger, but the Avenger had made it impossible for the Spider to pursue. But now that he could remain no longer, Wentworth would have to work like fury to find the Avenger and retrieve the weapon.

In order to escape from the trap, he had been forced to surrender into the Avenger's hands the weapon with which the Spider had killed. If the Avenger realized that, he need only send the automatic to police and his doom would be an accomplished fact. Also, if police checked the number on the automatic Wentworth had surrendered to the inspector and found it did not belong to Wentworth, there would be trouble. He made a mental note to recover the automatic at the first possible moment from the police. It was barely possible he might obtain a clue to the Avenger's identity through it, though he doubted that a man as clever as the masked one would leave such an easy and clear trail.

A policeman warming his back against a steam radiator in the apartment building's foyer saluted Wentworth with his club as he pushed out into the night. Instantly a car started down the line and Nita tooled it to the curb.

Wentworth did not speak. He slumped back in a corner of the seat, hands thrust into his pockets.

He was sure now that the Avenger had deliberately set into action a train of circumstances, all implicating the Spider at the scene of the kill. Nor did Wentworth believe that it had been done purely as a publicity stunt for the Avenger, though he seemed hungry enough for that type of fame. Criminals, even pseudo-Robin Hoods, did not recklessly attack the Spider for such reasons, even though there was a fifty-thousand dollar reward on his head. A sudden thought struck him: the Avenger's most spectacular activity had taken place on the same day those forty-three poison deaths had occurred. Was it possible...? Had the Avenger done that to reduce the publicity given to the poisonings?

Wentworth's head snapped up, his eyes narrowed. If that were so, the attack on himself must herald some incredible new visitation of death! Something that would pale those forty deaths into insignificance! The capture of the Spider would crowd all other news off the front pages of newspapers.

WENTWORTH CURSED raggedly, leaned forward and switched on the radio, fumbled for a station which he knew at this hour was broadcasting news reports. He listened with thoughtful cold eyes as the announcer's voice droned through a grist of featureless news: a ship had thrown a propeller off

Hatteras and been taken in tow by the Coast Guard Cutter *Mann;* two boys had broken through the ice of a skating pond and been drowned when they tried to rescue a pet dog… the car was drumming up West End Avenue, now yawing at the corners as the gusts swept up from the Hudson a block away. Nita braked to a halt as she caught a red light and the radio became suddenly louder.

"Here's a news flash," said the announcer. "Seventeen women have been rushed to the hospitals within the last hour, all with their faces terribly burned. Doctors said an acid apparently had been placed in some cosmetics. Many of the women will be permanently disfigured. For further details, read your local newspaper."

Wentworth smashed a clenched fist into his palm.

"That's it!" he said suddenly. "By God, that's it!"

"Heavens, Dick, what's the matter?" Nita asked fearfully. "It's a terrible thing, but…."

"That's more work of the poisoners," Wentworth said flatly. "And, by Heaven, the Avenger is helping them!"

There was a cold horror writhing within him. Seventeen women with their faces fearfully burned. Acid in cosmetics! But why? Why should any criminal do such a thing? What profit could he hope to gain from disfiguring women? From poisoning scores of people? Wentworth jerked his head angrily.

Certainly, this crime seemed to confirm his half-guess as to the Avenger's motives. What man would lend himself to such infamy? And what was the motive?

The car spun a corner to the left, bored through a howling

28

wind to Riverside Drive and coasted up to the entrance of a towering apartment building. Wentworth and Nita flung across the walk and into the foyer with a cold wind snapping at their heels. The rosy-cheeked hall boy recognized them by name and ushered them ceremoniously into the elevator with a swagger of incongruously wide shoulders. Despite the cold horror of this new crime, despite the turmoil in his mind, estimating motives, figuring his strategy against the Avenger, Wentworth felt a lift of his heart as the cage soared toward Nita's home.

A slight boyish smile curved Wentworth's lips, his eyes softened, turned a little wistful. All his love was Nita's; all her heart was his. Yet few were the hours they might share. His pledge of service to humanity had been made before they had met and he had fought against their love as if it were a shameful thing. For the Spider could never marry. How could he, with the threat of arrest and disgrace, of execution in the electric chair hanging ever over him? No man of honor could ask a woman to share such a life with him, nor think of having a home and children when any hour might bring him shameful doom.

But that love had proved stronger than the combined great strength of both of them. They had made concessions to their happiness. She should fight with him for the things he held dear. So that others might have happiness and be protected from the poisonous beast that was the underworld, these two denied themselves the solace of their love. Wentworth had never regretted his decision for an instant, but sometimes desire for a peaceful domestic life nearly overwhelmed him; sometimes the cup of life seemed unendurably bitter....

THE ELEVATOR boy flung wide the door and Wentworth stepped into the hall. He darted aside abruptly, his hand flying to the automatic holstered beneath his arm. But even as his fingers closed upon the butt, he checked himself, frowning.

A man had straightened away from the wall beside the door of Nita's apartment, a husky figure of a man in a shapeless overcoat and a crushed hat. The man shambled across toward him, lifting a hand to cover a yawn. "Good of you to come so soon, old pal," he said. "Have you a statement to make to a gentleman of the press?"

"What the hell—are you doing here, Blanton?" Wentworth demanded coldly.

The elevator boy stepped alertly into the hall. "Want me to throw him out, sir?" he asked brightly.

"How crude of you," the newspaper man murmured, but there was a hard glint in his eyes. It occurred to Wentworth that despite his slouch, Blanton was very husky and as large as the elevator boy. He refused with a curt shake of his head, a gesture of his hand that was dismissal. The elevator boy clicked a bow, stepped back into the cage and clanged the door.

"Now, Blanton," Wentworth said, "what do you want?"

Blanton had a blurred smile on his face, his eyes seemed sleepy, but there were shrewd wrinkles at their corners. His whole person was like that, careless and alert. His horsey face had a thin nose and his head was so narrow and long it seemed deformed. He smoked a cigarette in a holder at least twelve inches long.

"Wouldst have a word with thee," he said gently. "The city

editor cracked his whip over the phone at me, routed me out of the hay and bade me scamper over to intercept thee. I, not you, am the one who should wax exceedingly wroth. You weren't routed out of a downy bed…."

"What do you want?" Wentworth demanded again.

Blanton struck an attitude, left hand to his breast, right gesturing widely, but behind his mocking pantomime, his eyes never left Wentworth's keen face.

"Art angry with your little palsy?" His voice shuddered with mock horror.

Wentworth cursed impatiently and pushed past him toward the door of Nita's apartment. The reporter's hand rested lightly on Wentworth's arm and he peered with suddenly wide open eyes into his face.

"The Avenger says you are the Spider," Blanton said swiftly, clearly. "What statement have you in reply to that?"

Wentworth stopped and stared into the man's eyes. This play acting, this asinine behavior had not fooled him at all. He knew that Blanton had one of the shrewdest minds among the alert set of news men who gathered information for the New York dailies. He knew that Blanton was a clever psychologist, used to worming information from reluctant and defiant sources. He knew, too, that Blanton had looked upon him with suspicious eyes more than once when the Spider's activities had come to light. The Avenger was striking again, and even more viciously. Newspaper publicity of this sort would hamper Wentworth's movements enormously.

"He says he has positive proof—concrete evidence—that

you are the Spider," Blanton hammered on. "What have you to say, Wentworth?"

Wentworth smiled despite the sick thumping of his heart. The Avenger already had found out about the exchange of automatics! There could be no doubt as to his meaning. By Heaven, the man was shrewd! But why was he working this way, instead of turning the weapon over to police? Wentworth could not figure that, but he was sure that delay boded no good for the Spider. The Avenger undoubtedly was furthering some deep plan of his own.

Blanton's keen, sleepy eyes were studying Wentworth's face, but without profit. The secret services of the world had, on occasion, tried to pierce that mobile mask without success. Wentworth continued to smile. He reached out and pushed Blanton's chin with his palm so that the reporter's dinky, ridiculous hat slipped sideways on his head. There was just one defense, Wentworth knew, against the Avenger's round-about attack.

"Why say, Blanton," he told the reporter, gently mocking, "that the Avenger is absolutely correct. Of course, I'm the Spider!"

Wentworth threw back his head and laughed, heard Nita's smothered gasp. She stepped past and used her key. The reporter's eyes and mouth were wide open, ludicrous with surprise that was not all assumed. "May I print that?" he demanded eagerly.

Wentworth nodded graciously. "Certainly."

Blanton closed his mouth and glared at him. "You know damned well I can't print that!" he said savagely. "They'd laugh me out of the office if I phoned in anything like that. And I can't prove you said it."

Wentworth became apologetic. "I'm so sorry," he said. "I should have allowed the elevator boy to remain as a witness."

Wentworth bowed Nita through the opened door, waved a careless hand to Blanton.

"Come up'n see me sometime," Wentworth drawled. "And bring a witness!"

CHAPTER 4
THE SPIDER FALLS

THE DOOR closed behind Wentworth and his smile was instantly eclipsed. He faced Nita with a worried frown. A tawny, spotted Great Dane dog was prancing a boisterous welcome, but Wentworth greeted him only absently as they walked along the hall to the sprawling duplex living-room of Nita's apartment. A great studio window, with side drapes of warmly crimson velvet filled the entire side of the room, showed the black, wind-swept Hudson, the yellow lights of the Jersey shore. But Wentworth had no eyes for that, though there were times when his gaze turned wistful at the warm homey comfort of the apartment.

"What made you tell Eddie Blanton that?" Nita asked breathlessly. "Even if he can't print it…!"

Wentworth waved a hand wearily. "Blanton has been suspicious of me for a long time," he said. "I've seen it in his eyes when he hangs around Kirkpatrick's office. If I had denied it I would

33

have given countenance to the Avenger's charges. This way, Blanton is left without ammunition. He doesn't know whether I'm joking or not."

Wentworth took both Nita's hands in his, looking deeply into her violet eyes while he told her rapidly what had happened at Mannley's club. Nita's gaze was quiet and unafraid now. She was a poised woman of the world; her head of clustered chestnut curls was carried high and proudly; there was dignity as well as beauty in her face. Her brow bespoke wisdom, and clear courage was in the modeled firmness of her lips, a fitting mate for this Master of Men.

Wentworth finished his recital and she moved from him with a slow grace, bending over to light a laid fire on the hearth. The flames towered swiftly. Flickering red lights danced over her hair and found new life in its gleam, shadowed her gracious figure against the flowing lines of velvet gown, colored like wine.

"I'll have coffee for you in a moment, Dick," she said. "Some excellent brandy...."

Wentworth threw back his head and laughed sharply once. There was exhilaration, new life in the sound. Nita was always like this. In her he found a stimulus beyond belief. Her quiet courage spurred him to greater accomplishments. She smiled at him slowly now, the curve of her lips ineffably tender. Wentworth whirled, crossed the room with long, bouncing strides to a dressing room and a wardrobe behind a secret panel which held, behind a row of his own correct clothing, the garbs of his disguises. They were only a fraction of what filled the closets of his own Fifth Avenue apartment, but many times he had found it impossible to go there, had needed to draw upon this secondary depot.

"Nita, dear," he called. "Would you phone Ram Singh please to rent a coupé and get here as swiftly as he can?"

While he asked her to summon his faithful Hindu body servant, he was busy before a mirror that was framed in white neon lights, constructing over his own firm, vital face, the sallow countenance of the Spider. The nose, built up with putty, became sharp and beak-like, the skin tautened until it emphasized the high cheek bones. Bushy thick eyebrows covered the suave line of his own. He draped a cloak over his arm, selected a wide-brimmed black slouch hat and thrust into a pocket a wig of lank long hair. Then he strode back into the living-room.

Nita came toward him with a china saucer in her hands. Her face was ashen as she held it out. A bit of gold chain lay in a pat of white greasy cream. Green bubbles stood up all over the chain and stained the grease.

"I bought a fresh jar of cold cream today," Nita said in a slightly muffled voice. "After I heard that radio broadcast, I thought I'd better test it."

Wentworth stared down at the green mess which the acid, acting on the copper in the chain, had made of the cold cream. His eyes lifted to Nita's dear face and a shudder shook him as he envisioned it welted and destroyed by the work of that acid.

"Thank God you tried it first!" he cried hoarsely.

THEIR EYES met and Nita set the saucer down and crept into his arms. Wentworth stared straight before him over her dear head. Seventeen women had been scarred for life by the

The Avenger pivoted and slammed
his fist full into Wentworth's face!

work of these fiends tonight. Nita had barely escaped. What in
God's name could be the motive behind such horror?

With an effort, Wentworth threw off the bitter anger that
rose within him. When he spoke, his voice was flat and edged:

"I'm going to pay Patsy Malone a visit," he said briefly. "You
remember the girl who got Jackson in a jam with the Avenger?

I'm positive that through her I can get a lead to the Avenger. I've got to find him. If he isn't responsible for these… these horrors, I must know it so that I can hunt the true trail… And I must recover my automatic and destroy it. Never before has such damaging evidence got into hostile hands. I'm afraid…."

The hall boy rang from below and reported that Ram Singh had arrived with the car. Wentworth clasped Nita in his arms. Her hand stole across his shoulders, her fingers twined in his hair. A moment of happiness then Wentworth was gone, the disguised face that alone was changed now, half-hidden in a silken muffler.

Eddie Blanton pulled his shoulders loose from the wall and ambled toward him, hands buried in the sagging pockets of his top coat.

"Give us a break, Wentworth," he urged. "Give me a serious answer for my paper."

Wentworth turned his back to him, stood facing the elevator door. "I'm tired of answering such fool charges," he said coldly. "Your paper would do better to ask the Avenger what he has done with the loot he hijacked from various crooks. Why is it that every time he pulls something especially spectacular and grabs off the entire front page of the newspaper, some other heinous crime is committed? Such as the disfiguring of those seventeen women today!"

"What do you mean, Wentworth?" Blanton was strangely excited, crowding up close beside him now, trying to peer into his face. The elevator door opened and Wentworth strode in, sent Blanton backwards with a swift thrust at his chest.

"Down," he ordered the boy shortly.

"Right you are, sir!" The boy slammed the door alertly, the roses of his cheeks redder than ever with excitement. The elevator swooped downward, while the signal buzzed continuously for the floor of Nita's apartment. It rang all the way down to the first floor.

"I'll take care of him, sir," the boy promised, with a slight straightening of his wide shoulders.

Wentworth said, "Never mind." He tipped the boy and strode out to the small coupé that Ram Singh held at the curb. The wind smacked him in the face and he grabbed his lifting hat, ducked into the car. The Hindu set it instantly in motion.

"Men from the newspapers have been at the house, *sahib*," he reported, his dark, hawkish face impassive. "They wish to know the *sahib's* answer to this pig of a pretender, this Avenger, who accuses the *sahib*."

Wentworth nodded thoughtfully. Whether the Avenger was trying to trap him, or merely to handicap him in his fight against the poison killers, he had taken a clever way. If the Avenger made out a strong enough case, newspaper men would dog his movements for days, might even set detectives on his trail. A heavy frown roughened his forehead. He must not be hampered. So many lives depended on his freedom to fight the poisoners.

Absently, he removed his hat, drew into place the lank, long wig he carried in his pocket, and cloaked his shoulders in a long, black cape. The coupé left Riverside Drive behind and let the wind blow it up Ninety-sixth street across the dimmer lights of upper Broadway. Minutes later, it drew to a halt near a red brick tenement. Wentworth spoke briefly to Ram Singh in Hindu-stani, caught the acquiescent nod of the Hindu's turbaned head, his murmured, *"Han, Sahib."*

It was the Spider who alighted from the coupé, a hunch-backed figure in a wind-flapped cape that shuffled his awkward way with deceptive swiftness along the sidewalk. A moment only was he visible; then the street held only a parked coupé and the sound of cold whining wind.

In the shadows of a dimly lighted hall, a twisted, sinister shadow moved. The Spider went with soundless speed and paused presently before a doorway. Behind it a tinny radio blasted music but only made the quiet of the hall more oppres-sive. Despite the noisy instrument, the apartment within seemed still also—still with a waiting tension....

A TIGHT smile made faint lines about the Spider's lipless mouth. Was this the next trap of the Avenger? Had he figured that Wentworth would follow him here? Slowly, the Spider nodded. Oh, the man was clever! Wentworth faded away from that doorway and the black shadow drifted up another floor, and another until he could reach the scuttle and gain the roof.

From a compact tool-kit that he carried strapped always beneath his left arm, Wentworth drew a length of silken cord. It was scarcely as thick as a pencil, yet such was its cunning weave, and of such high quality were its fibers that it could lift seven hundred pounds.

With practiced speed, Wentworth looped the cord about a chimney pot, threw its two ends over into space and, twisting the doubled line about his arms and legs, lowered himself with swift ease into the darkness of an air-shaft.

The winds of the heavens swept overhead and swirled down into the black pit. The Spider's cape swirled and flapped about him like the wings of a giant bat. But he steadied his body with feet touching the brick walls and went steadily downward until he was at the level of the apartment at whose door he had listened. Still that tinny radio shrieked and vibrated and still he could feel that tense waiting. A green shade full of tiny pinpricks of light covered the window.

Only one other window was lighted. It was a story below where he swung, across the areaway. Through it, he could see a girl before a dressing table mirror. She patted grease from a jar into her face. Wentworth bit his lips to keep from shouting a warning. Silly, of course. There wasn't one chance in a hundred that the girl had got hold of one of the acid-tainted jars. But she was so young, her face so fresh. Wentworth jerked his head in negation. No, he could not warn her lest he betray his presence. He was being foolish. Her cold cream was safe.

Still his eyes clung with fascination to the scene. The girl had pulled off her dress and wore a pale, sleazy slip of green that left her young plump shoulders bare. She stretched her neck, pointing her chin at the mirror as she worked the grease in thoroughly. Abruptly she stopped, her finger tips just touching her cheek. She frowned at her reflection in the mirror, felt her flesh in bewilderment.

Her face twisted in pain. She snatched a cloth and began to

rub frantically, swabbing off the grease. She sprang to her feet. Through the glass window, Wentworth heard her cry out.

"Oh, God!" she screamed. She was dancing with pain now and Wentworth cursed with stiffly rigid lips. He knew, even if that girl down there did not, what had happened. Once more, the acid-laden cosmetics had struck. He saw a man dash up to the girl, heard her screaming words, then the man snatched her from his vision. Wentworth cursed with slow, thick-throated violence. If only he had warned her! But he knew that he could not. White rage burned within him, rage at these fiends who struck at innocent women. This was not murder. It was lifetime torture that was being inflicted. Pain, then the horror of a welted, hideous face.

Lights began to spring up on the other side of the airshaft. A window directly opposite blossomed yellow. The Spider must move if he would escape detection. It was significant that the window shade already drawn down had not been raised. He was positive now that the Avenger lurked behind it. If that Hooded One was responsible for these horrors that had been inflicted this night, heaven help him....

Stiff with cold, the Spider got a foothold on the window sill, ducked his face into his arms and pushed himself violently out into the air shaft. He swung out three feet. He jerked up his knees to protect body and tight gripped hands and went through the window with a smash and a tinkle of broken glass. The spring roller of the green shade tripped and it slapped upward with a noisy, dying flutter. Wentworth landed on his feet, flung himself to the right until his shoulders struck a wall, and came out of his crouch with a gun in each fist.

"Stay just like you are," he ordered sharply.

Beside the closed door, the bulky hooded figure of the Avenger crouched, hand frozen half-way to his gun. On a rickety iron bed on the far side of the room a girl and a boy crouched miserably and in a chair a round-faced man hugged a baby against his chest.

Wentworth needed only a glance to know that the girl was the Patsy Malone whom Jackson had described, five-feet-two of tobasco. Danger signals were flying in her cheeks and in the bright anger of her blue eyes. The husky blond kid beside her must be the younger brother, the man with the baby must be a neighbor.

WENTWORTH'S EYES narrowed on a slip of paper clenched between the boy's fingers, a slip of pink paper that was a check. The Devil! Had the Avenger played philanthropist and given the forged check back to the boy?

His quick question brought a wondering nod from the boy. One thing to mark up to the Avenger's credit then, but it could not change Wentworth's plans.

"Avenger!" he snapped. "You're coming with me. To the window, quickly."

The hooded, blank face with eyes glittering through the slits confronted him without words. The man was still crouched with his hand half-way to his gun.

"Quickly," Wentworth repeated, "or the police will take us both."

A sound like dry laughter came from behind the mask. "You have more to fear from police than I, Spider," said the Avenger grimly. "Let us wait for them."

Wentworth cursed, stalked swiftly toward the Avenger, a blackjack dangling from his left wrist while the automatic in his right held his prisoner motionless. He caught a quick movement to his left, saw that the blond youth was charging toward him in a head-down, desperate run!

"Get back!" Wentworth warned desperately. He didn't want to hurt the boy, but….

His dodge was too late. Young Malone slammed into him. The boy was powerful and sent him reeling, even as he struck with the blackjack. Patsy Malone cried out. The bed creaked as she leaped into the fight. The Avenger got his gun in his hand. Once more he laughed and came forward lightly, his heavy shoulders rolled forward in readiness to strike.

He was almost within striking distance when Wentworth finally fought clear of Shane Malone and allowed the boy to slump to the floor. The Avenger's gun was lifted to crash against the Spider's skull, but Wentworth was ready for him. He flung up his weapon to put a bullet through his assailant's arm, then hesitated. He could hit the Avenger's arm without difficulty. His perfection of aim assured that, but the bullet would plough on through, and behind the Avenger crouched the man with the baby in his arms.

Wentworth's hesitation undid him. The Avenger's gun raked out and struck him numbingly on the head. As he reeled backward, still hesitating to shoot on account of the baby, Patsy Malone flung herself upon him.

Dazedly, he heard a curse rip out from the doorway, heard the door slam inward and jerked his head about. A uniformed policeman stood on the threshold, revolver ready.

"Stop it!" he roared. "Hands up, the lot of youse!"

But Patsy Malone was past heeding him and Wentworth could not help himself. The girl flung herself upon him, sent him stumbling backward. Her clawing hands raked his face. Her light-slippered feet kicked at his shins.

"You've killed Shane," she cried. "You've killed Shane!"

Wentworth's head was beginning to clear. His eyes made a swift survey of the room as he went backward. The Avenger had whirled to face the door, his hands rising, his gun falling to the floor.

"That man is Spider!" The Avenger's deep voice rang out. "I am Avenger and I was taking him prisoner to turn over to police!"

THE POLICEMAN'S stride carried him almost within reach of the Avenger. Wentworth flung an arm about Patsy Malone and flopped down on his back, pulling her with him. As he fell, he hurled his blackjack upward and the lights crashed out. The policeman was silhouetted against a dim rectangle of flickering gas illumination in the hall, but the rest of them were in shadow.

With a heave of his body, Wentworth tossed Patsy aside. He sprawled forward to snatch the Avenger's gun from the floor and saw the Hooded Man go forward, heard his fist thud and the policeman reel back. The Spider was off like a sprinter from his mark. As the policeman hit the door jamb, bounced and measured his length on the floor, Wentworth reached the Avenger and ground the automatic into the small of his back.

"Down the stairs fast!" the Spider ordered. His voice was low and there was steel in it.

The Avenger hesitated, then with a guttural curse moved toward the steps. Sharp heels beat the floor explosively behind Wentworth.

He reached out to strike down the Avenger, to whirl toward this new menace, but he was too late. A woman's arms, Patsy Malone's, flung around his throat from behind.

"Run, Avenger! Run!" she panted.

The Avenger pivoted and slammed his fist full in Wentworth's helpless face. He went down and carried the girl with him and the Avenger's feet beat a hurried retreat down the steps. Patsy Malone scrambled erect, her breath coming fast. The Spider lay where he had fallen, unconscious. Patsy scooped up the pistol and held it in a trembling hand.

The timid, round-faced man, with the baby still clutched in his arms, stuck his head out of her apartment door.

"It's all right, Mr. Coxwell," Patsy said, somewhat scornfully. "The Spider is unconscious."

"F-f-fine!" stammered the man. "Keep him that way while I run for another policeman!"

CHAPTER 5
THE AVENGER PLOTS

WHILE WENTWORTH lay unconscious, the Avenger made good his swift flight. He raced down the stairs, out through the back and into the next street through another tenement. As he passed through the second building, be removed his hat and yanked the masking hood from his head shoved, it into a pocket. Then he pulled the brim of his black hat low over his eyes, ducked his head and plowed along into the cold wind.

Two blocks farther along the street, he entered a parked sedan, climbed in under the wheel and waited. He drew out a tobacco pouch and, with a large piece of paper, made what the Russians call a "goat's ankle," a cigarette that held as much tobacco as a pipe. He lighted that, chuckled once as he blew out a great cloud of smoke. He wore only a light suit coat, yet he did not seem to find the frigid, still air of the sedan cold. He chuckled again as if there were something rarely amusing in his thoughts.

It was five minutes later that a second man, clad exactly like himself except that he wore a long cape cloak, opened the door, slid into the car.

"All goes well, Ivan?" the man asked, pronouncing the name *Ee-ván* in the Russian manner.

"All goes very well, Master," the man with the "goat's ankle" between his lips agreed, and reported rapidly what had occurred in the Malone apartment.

"Good!" exclaimed the Master. "I have one more little errand for you tonight, Ivan. Take care of the O'Burke affair tonight. I'll phone the papers and the police can mark another crime as 'solved by the Avenger.'"

Both men laughed together. The interior of the sedan was thick with the smoke of Ivan's malodorous cigarette, the windows were misting over. Ivan puffed again, seemed to hesitate.

"Master," he said finally, "that is one thing I do not understand. Why did you have me kill O'Burke? He is a gang leader from Chicago, and you...."

"I am giving orders," the Avenger. "It is your part to obey."

His voice was cold as the moan of the wind in the street. "This arrangement was your suggestion when I saved you from the police after you committed murder. You said your life was mine and that you would serve me faithfully in all things, even if you didn't know who I was, or why I did things."

"That is true, Master," Ivan said quickly, and his words were abject. "I do not question. My life is yours. I serve you as I would my chieftain upon steppes." His head was bowed before the burning regard of the eyes behind the mask.

"See that you remember it," the Avenger said harshly. "Tomorrow night," he went on, "you go to Chicago. I have heard that a rare shipment of diamonds has been received there, and I should like to add some of them to my collection. I don't believe any of the crooks out there would tackle it, so you'll take three men west from New York and I'll join you later. When you have the diamonds turn loose a narcotic bomb. Tie up your three companions and leave them to take the rap. Be careful you don't betray your identity."

Ivan nodded slowly. "You may trust me, Master."

If Wentworth could have heard their unemotional plotting to steal a fortune in gems and leave other criminals as prisoners to take the blame, his eyes would have blazed at confirmation of one theory. But the Avenger was going even farther than Wentworth suspected. He was no hijacking crook. He was committing the crime himself, then leaving the innocent to take the blame! Small wonder that he had no difficulty in solving crimes! But there was as yet no mention of that horror of which Wentworth suspected the Avenger—the poisonings and the injury of women.

The Master studied Ivan in the semi-darkness of the car. Their faces were not visible, save that the glow of the "goat's ankle" gleamed momentarily on the Russian's high cheek bones, revealed a thin-bridged nose; revealed, too, that even while talking to his man, the one addressed as Master wore the hood of the Avenger.

HE SAT silently for a while, staring at the misted windshield which showed the street beyond only dimly. Things were progressing very satisfactorily. The Spider by this time must have been taken prisoner either by that policeman who lay unconscious beside him, or by other police whom the Malones had summoned. The news of his capture, coupled with the O'Burke affair would be smashed all over the front pages of the newspapers in the morning.

His fame would be greater than ever. That little Robin Hood

trick of gifts to the poor had caught the imagination of the people and he was in small danger of capture by the police. At any time they closed in on him he need only to flee into someone's home and tell them he was the Avenger. They would hide him. Was not the Avenger the friend of the people?

Tonight had been a fair sample of that. Because Ivan had returned the check to Shane Malone, the boy and Patsy had knocked over the Spider for him. Ah, yes, these little philanthropies paid good dividends. A low dry laugh filtered through his black mask. His hand dropped to the handle of the door.

"Carry on, Ivan," he said lightly. "You have done good work tonight. That motion picture you took of the Spider killing that gambler, Mannley, turned out perfectly. It is too bad he was in disguise, but I think I have a way of solving that difficulty. The film should be in the hands of police in less than an hour." He paused, working the door handle up and down. It made a slight squeaking. "I'll look for you at the usual place in about four hours. We prepare that little excursion to Chicago."

"Master…" The Russian hesitated, held the last short fragment of his cigarette pinched between his fingers. "Master, who are these people who are killing many others with poison in tinned meat? Who are burning the faces off women with acid? Do you know, Master? It seems to me that they are very powerful, that we would better be careful lest we cross them."

The Avenger nodded slowly. "They are powerful," he agreed, soberly, then laughed suddenly. "Perhaps there may be some profit in that for us also."

The door clicked open and he stepped to the pavement. "I must make sure that the Spider does not escape."

Ivan coaxed the cold motor into life and drove rapidly southward, cut through an underpass beneath Central Park and pushed on toward the East River. Before a slatternly tenement, he parked the car. Five minutes later, he returned with a bundle over his shoulder—a bundle wrapped in burlap that was about five feet, six inches long and which squirmed with an independent life.

Ivan opened the rear door of the sedan, dumped the bundle roughly to the floor where it squirmed and made muffled groanings. Then he drove on. He came at length to a dim gray building about which the winds soughed mournfully, whose only light issued dimly from a cavernous door and served only to make the rest of the building, the tall barred windows, more dreary. Into the doorway, Ivan trudged with his now motionless bundle. And over Ivan's face had been drawn the black hood of the Avenger which showed nothing but the steely glitter of his eyes.

He leaned heavily on the bell and stood against the door so that the bundle on his shoulder concealed his masked face, but so that he could peer into the interior. From the doorway, a high, dim hall ran straight back to twin wooden doors that were black. On each side of the corridor was another doorway. It was from the opening to the right that a bent old man wearing a uniform cap issued presently. He carried a large ring of keys in his left hand and in his right was a flashlight. Ivan jabbed the bell twice more impatiently, raising an echoing clangor within. The old man called something in a cracked voice and his shuffle became a little more rapid. He peered out, flashing his light so that it made a round white disc on the thick glass of the door. It was possible now to make out the metal legend that was attached to the front of his uniform cap. It read:

CITY MORGUE

THE OLD man made querulous noises behind the glass and Ivan shook the door with an impatient hand. Finally the keeper shrugged and opened the door a crack. Instantly Ivan's shoulder swung it violently wide and he jammed a gun against the man's ribs.

"You will not be hurt," he said harshly, "if you obey. I am Avenger."

The old man reeled back with fright in his eyes. The door jarred shut behind the Avenger and his bundle began to make muffled sounds again.

"Quickly," said the Avenger. "Take me to the place where they've put O'Burke's body."

"What… what do you want?" the old man quavered. "There ain't nothing here except corpses. What's that you got in your bundle?"

"Hurry!" rasped the hooded man. "O'Burke's body!" He thrust the pistol menacingly forward. The old man stumbled down the hall, casting fearful glances back over his shoulder and the Avenger crowded close on his heels. His arm was clamped tightly about his bundle and its squirmings did not inconvenience him in the least.

Slowly the queer procession moved down the dim corridor,

feet making flat echoes through the empty building. At the big double doors, the old keeper hesitated a moment, fumbling with his keys, then he inserted one in the lock and leaned against the door. He giggled nervously as it swung inward and he switched on lights.

"Reckon it don't make no difference to *them*," he mumbled. "And they do say you don't hurt folks, Mr. Avenger."

He shuffled across the tile floor. There was a damp chill in the air and the wailing of the wind crept into the room. Their footsteps seemed a violation of something that was both sacred and terrible. The thin, bent, old keeper giggled again, sucking his toothless gums.

"O'Burke won't mind neither," he cackled. "He may have been a hell of a big shot, but he's just a number now. Two-eighty-three."

Along the wall, chest high, ran a wide cabinet of white porcelain. In it were two tiers of deep drawers and over each was a small brass plate with a number on it. The keeper flashed his light on one or two of these, pointed a knotted old finger at one.

"In there," he said.

He turned toward the masked man behind him, then he let out a thin squeal and flattened against the chests. The Avenger's gun thudded on his old head and the keeper slumped to the floor. Ivan grunted and dumped his bundle down, caught hold of the handle of drawer 283 and pulled.

The drawer slid straight out and a gust of cold came with it from the refrigeration plant that kept those drawers, and their contents, at icy temperatures. The drawer was without sides, a white porcelain slab. On it a man's nude body and in his chest were four bullet holes. The Morgue keeper was right. O'Burke wouldn't care about anything any more.

For a long moment, the Avenger stood look down at the body on the slab, then he bent over his bundle and unwrapped it, spilled out a man who was wrapped in rope like a cocoon, whose mouth was stopped by a tight white gag. Swiftly the Avenger removed the gag. With it, he bound the man by his neck to the thigh of O'Burke's corpse.

"What… what are you doing to me?" the bound captive demanded. He had a childish face, warped by childish cruelty. His mental age could not have been above seven, but the dissipation that marred his countenance could not have been acquired in less than thirty years.

"What are you doing to me?" he demanded again, twisting his neck to see behind him.

"I'm tying you to O'Burke's corpse," said the Avenger, with a chuckle.

He drew an automatic from his pocket, holding it in a handkerchief, and deposited it in the bound man's lap.

"That's the gun you killed him with," he went on. "Your fingerprints are on it."

A squeal of terror gasped from the man's lips. "I… I didn't kill O'Burke," he shrieked. "You can't do this to me. You can't!"

Once more the Avenger chuckled. "I know you didn't kill him," he said, "because it happens I did, and with that gun. But the weapon is yours. You bought it two months ago. Your fingerprints are on the butt. Also you are member of rival mob. I think police will convict you of crime all right. This note—" he tied it deftly to the trigger guard of the gun—"will give them details."

"For God's sake, Avenger!" the man gabbed. "Don't do it! Don't...!"

The Avenger stepped back and surveyed his handiwork, the man with the young-old face, tied by his throat to the thigh of O'Burke's corpse; the automatic in his lap and the aged morgue keeper sprawled unconscious beside him. He chuckled again, turned on his heel and stalked from the room while the bound man shrieked and shrieked.

Within an hour, the papers would chant forth once more the praises of the Avenger. With his uncanny knowledge of the underworld, he had solved another crime that baffled police, found the murderer of that mighty gang leader, O'Burke from Chicago.

CHAPTER 6
"THIS IS THE END"

WHILE THE Avenger went about his mysterious business, Wentworth lay unconscious upon the floor of the hall beside the policeman the Avenger had slugged. Patsy Malone, standing over him with the automatic in her hand, glanced anxiously at their supine bodies, turned her worried blue eyes toward the door of her apartment.

"Shane!" she called urgently. "Shane!"

No reply came from the darkness. The girl became anxious. She glanced down at the bodies of the hall again and neither moved. The girl turned and ran into the apartment. "Shane! Shane!" she called again.

In the hall was no movement save the shifting of shadows from the wind-blown gas jet. The two men, Spider and policeman, lay side by side and did not stir. Shrill voices made an excited gabble below. Tenants had heard the sounds of struggle. They were uncertain what had occurred or where it had happened.

Pasty Malone hurried back into the hall, called down the stairwell: "Get a doctor!" she cried. "Go get Doctor Simmons. Shane is hurt!"

A man's voice shouted an answer and Patsy Malone turned back to stare down at the two bodies, the gun ready. Leaning her hips against the railing, she was a small, worried girl. There was a vertical pucker between her arched brows. Her black curling hair was disheveled and she brushed it up off her forehead with an impatient wrist. A tremor tugged at her chin, but she set her lips stubbornly. She began to walk up and down the hall, four short steps toward the head of the stairs, four short steps back. Her movements were light and graceful.

A low groan from one of the men stopped her, poised and alert, the automatic jerking up. The sound was not repeated and presently she resumed her anxious pacing. Feet pounded on the steps and Coxwell's ruddy, round face showed in the stairwell. He stopped, staring down at the two men.

"You took long enough," Pasty said tartly.

"I couldn't find a cop," Coxwell's breath was short. "I stopped by home to leave Junior, then I couldn't find a cop. I called them up finally and they wanted my life history before they'd send a radio car around…."

"But they're coming?" Patsy demanded.

"They're coming," Coxwell nodded.

The words echoed like his own knell in the ears of the Spider. He had regained consciousness a few seconds before and had tested Patsy's alertness with a groan. He did not like the competent way in which she handled that automatic. She would know how to use it and even an excited woman could hardly miss him at this distance. But he must find a way out. If he were captured in this disguise, police would need no damning automatic pistol to convict him of murder.

He studied the scene beneath lowered lids. Perhaps, the policeman beside him would regain consciousness first and distract them—give Wentworth his chance. But it would have to be soon. Radio patrolmen traveled fast. It could not be many moments before the men showed up. The sound of tumbling feet gave Wentworth a brief chance to hope. But it was very brief. Shane Malone staggered drunkenly into the hall. When he saw Wentworth, supine upon the floor, he dropped the hands that gripped his aching head and slammed his foot heavily against Wentworth's side.

"You louse!" he growled, and drew back his foot again.

Wentworth stiffened his muscles. He must not wince. He must take this blow without flinching or he would betray the fact that he had recovered consciousness and all chance of tricking Patsy Malone and escaping would be lost. In his mind, he

57

could imagine already the eager clamor of the newspapers over his capture, the boastful words of the Avenger.

"Stop it, Shane," Patsy ordered sharply. "There's no sense in kicking a man when he's down."

Shane grumbled, but he desisted and Wentworth had hard work to suppress a sigh of relief. The boy reeled toward the steps, muttering something about a drink and Coxwell stood over the Spider.

"You haven't tied him up," he said, his voice quaking.

"You do it," Patsy ordered. "I don't want to get close to him with this gun. He might be shamming unconsciousness."

WENTWORTH'S EYES glinted beneath the lowered lids. That young woman knew tactics. But her efficiency meant his own doom. If he were bound, he would have no chance at all of getting away before police arrived on the scene. He must not be bound. He simply must not! But what chance did he have, flat on his back this way, with that gun keeping watch? He must act and act quickly. Deep in his throat, Wentworth groaned. He rolled his head. If he could persuade Coxwell to make a hasty attempt to tie him up… Damn it! Coxwell was shrinking back, rather than advancing.

"Hurry!" Patsy snapped. "Tie him up. I won't be able to hold him after he comes to. He's slippery. Hurry, I tell you!"

Coxwell hung back a moment, then dropped on his knees and began to fumble with Wentworth's belt to use on his wrists. As he bent over, the Spider's arms jerked upward and clamped about his neck. Coxwell uttered a strangled cry, tried to heave erect. He was a big man, wide-shouldered and strong and his jerk flung him to his feet, dragging Wentworth with him. His fists slammed against the Spider's sides, hammered his breath out in gusts between set teeth.

Wentworth had counted too much on the man's fear. Apparently, Coxwell was brave enough when he was cornered and his big fists were scoring painfully. And Wentworth was handicapped. He must keep Coxwell between his body and Patsy's automatic.

He wrestled Coxwell about so that together they blocked the hall. Patsy, hovering behind the big man with her automatic raised and ready, found it impossible to shoot. Abruptly, the Spider slammed the crown of his head under Coxwell's chin. The big man straightened with a grunt, went limp.

Instantly, Wentworth seized the rail with both hands, vaulted over to the steps. He landed in a sprawl half-way down to the floor below, twisted an ankle painfully. Men and women broke and ran screaming as he thudded. Patsy called out a sharp order to halt.

Wentworth seized the rail and vaulted again, landing in the hall and putting the ceiling between himself and that threatening gun. He almost cried out with pain in his ankle but he could not pause. Only one flight of stairs now was between himself and the safety of the street. He hurried painfully along, limping to favor his twisted ankle, darted down the last stairs.

Brakes squealed at the front door and two bounding figures in blue uniform plunged up the steps from the street. Wentworth cursed and spun toward the rear. A tall man in his undershirt stood there, gripping a heavy iron poker in both hands. As the

Spider plunged toward him, he whipped it up over his head. But he had miscalculated the height of the ceiling. The poker struck, jarring his hands, breaking his swing. Before he could set himself again, Wentworth sprang upon him.

His right fist smashed home and the man reeled against the wall, not out, but momentarily dazed. Wentworth caught him by his shoulders and whirled him into the middle of the hall. While the man still swayed there, he pounded on toward the rear exit of the tenement. The police shouted excited warnings, but that hulking figure in the middle of the hall kept them from firing. **WENTWORTH DIVED** out the door, reached a fence in a bound and gripping its top, flung himself over. As he landed, he whistled shrilly three times. It was a piercing sound that would carry a long way. It would signal Ram Singh to get the car under way, to look for him when he burst to the street and be ready for a quick getaway.

Wentworth whirled toward the next tenement, racing through it toward the front while the police pounded through the other building toward the back. He knew that other police cars must be racing to the scene. A half-dozen at least would be sent if Coxwell had told them the Spider was stretched unconscious on the floor of the building. But for moments, the way would be clear, and with Ram Singh to pick him up from a flying start....

He burst out of the front door, poised in the darkness while his glance swept the street for the coupé. It was nowhere in sight!

A harsh curse tore Wentworth's throat. He whirled toward the back of the building and heard heavy feet hit the floor. A policeman had climbed the fence in his wake. He swung out of the front door, leaping to the pavement.

"Hands up!" The order was howled from the other tenement.

Wentworth spun that way, looked down the barrel of a revolver held tensely in a policeman's hand. It was a moment for quick thought and quicker action. Within seconds, the other policeman would reinforce the first. Within minutes, other police cars would rocket into the street. And to be captured in the garb of the Spider meant death as surely as if those robes were lined with poisoned needles. Yet Wentworth could not use lethal weapons against the police. For all his lawlessness, for all his death-dealing to criminals, he had never fired on protectors of the law.

Nevertheless, his hand flashed toward his underarm holster and he cursed defiance of the policeman. The officer's face hardened, his hand contracted and the revolver belched flame and lead straight at Wentworth, who cried out in a choked voice, diving to the pavement, his legs jerking convulsively.

"I got him!" the cop yelled. "I killed the Spider!"

He sprang to Wentworth's side, caught him by the shoulder. Wentworth's arm flew out and the man's legs shot from under him. He came down hard and the Spider's fist, the rolling weight of his body, met his jaw. Then Wentworth was up and sprinting down the street. The police car was at the curb, but he ignored that, except to shoot off a tire as he raced past.

He had played a hair-breadth game and had won. When he had gone for his gun, it had been for the sole purpose of forcing the policeman to shoot. The hardening of the man's face, the inevitable tightening of the mouth and eyes that betrayed the decision to shoot, had been sufficient warning. Wentworth had gone down with the flash instead of after it. His head had gone down under the bullet in the instant the policeman fired. A hole ripped in the back brim of his hat, a furrow across his shoulder burned by the same bullet bore witness to the closeness of his escape.

Behind him, a gunshot whip-cracked through the cold night and lead sang shrilly past his ear. Two more strides, once more the whimpering song of lead and he went around the corner with a bullet hole in the flapping tail of his cape. Seconds later, a radio car skated around the corner on hot rubber, roared toward the tenement. Wentworth spurted into a second cross street, loped on for another block and, changing his direction a third time, dropped to a walk, his chest pumping. He felt prickles of heat over his entire body at the narrowness of his escape and once more he was aware of the pain in his ankle. He limped heavily onward.

TWICE NOW he had tangled with the Avenger, and the man had slipped from his grasp. He was no nearer knowledge of him now than he had been before, no nearer testing his theory of a connection between the man and the horrors that had been loosed on the city. That girl whose tormented screams rang now in his memory would be disfigured for life, her fresh youthful beauty ruined. Nita had barely escaped.

Mounting within him, Wentworth felt the familiar tide of white wrath against these unscrupulous criminals who preyed upon the innocent. He had foiled a hundred plots, sent a thousand criminals to their deaths, but still the wanton killing went on. Always some new monster lifted his head, devised some new means of squeezing money from the people by means of death and torture and mawkish terror.

Wentworth still felt convinced that the Avenger was in some way tied up with this new attack, but he had been stopped at every point in his efforts to make sure. He must turn from the pursuit of this phantom, pick up the direct trail of these poisoners—these destroyers of women's beauty. Such clues to the Avenger as remained must be followed by Jackson and Ram Singh while he turned to the trail of the poisoners.

But where was Ram Singh? Wentworth had left his faithful Hindu with implicit directions to remain ready for a quick getaway, yet the car and his man had been gone when he most needed them. Either Ram Singh had been seized, or… By heaven, that must be it! Ram Singh must have seen the Avenger fleeing the scene of their conflict, figured that his departure meant the end of danger for the Spider and followed the man!

Eagerly, Wentworth sought a dark doorway and divested himself of the main part of his disguise, shrugged the hunch from his shoulders and sought a phone. If Ram Singh had picked up a trail, he would communicate at once with Jenkyns, the aged butler at Wentworth's Fifth Avenue apartment. That was standard procedure. Eagerly, Wentworth put through his call.

"Yes, sir," Jenkyns dignified old voice reported. "Ram Singh phoned. He said he had struck a hot trail and would call again."

Wentworth's step was buoyant as he left the phone-booth and

took a taxi to his apartment. Perhaps after all, he was to have one more chance to try conclusions with this Hooded Man whom all the city idolized, whom the Spider alone suspected of duplicity. The new Negro operator of his private elevator smiled slowly, showing his white teeth, as he bowed Wentworth into the car and sent it smoothly upward fifteen stories to his penthouse.

"Lots of folks ask for you tonight, sir," the boy reported in his slow drawl. "Mr. Kirkpatrick upstairs. I shooed a lot of newspaper men away."

Wentworth nodded with a frown, his mind flicking back to the automatic that the Avenger still held, the automatic that would identify Richard Wentworth as the Spider and a murderer. Wentworth felt his muscles tightening, knew that subconsciously he had thrown himself upon the balls of his feet as if prepared for flight or battle. Had he escaped police and the Avenger, only to have Kirkpatrick come for him with the evidence to condemn him?

SLOWLY, WENTWORTH fought the tension from his breast, made his muscles relax. He did not want to question the operator, but he had said that Kirkpatrick was in his apartment and had not mentioned other police. Kirkpatrick would not have come alone if an arrest was intended. Furthermore, there had been no furtive shadows on the street to close in on his flanks. No, he was allowing his fears to betray him.

The operator slid open the door and Wentworth tightened again, feeling muscles quiver throughout his body as he spotted four men waiting in the hall before his door. Then he recognized them as newspapermen and he made his step nonchalant as he left the cage.

"Get out of here, bums," he said, and felt that his smile was obviously forced. He could not immediately shake off the fears that had gripped him.

The four men sighed in unison. "So you decided to come home at last?" one, a tall, hatless skeleton of a man jeered. "Come on, now, Wentworth, what you got to say about the Avenger? You know, the claims you're the Spider."

"No statement, boys," Wentworth said crisply. He stepped to his door, thumbed the bell button. He was frowning while the news men clamored about him. He could not operate effectively with all these men hounding him. Everywhere he turned, a newspaper man bobbed up at his elbow. They were keeping too close tabs on his movements, playing into the Avenger's hands.

Surveillance was the last thing in the world he wanted now. He must be free to operate against the poisoners, against the acid-destroyers. God alone knew how many more would be stricken if he did not strike at the criminals. His eyes narrowed angrily as a small, earnest youth with an excited gleam in his eyes thrust between him and the door.

"You can't defy the press like this, Mr. Wentworth," he said earnestly. "The people have a right to know the truth."

Wentworth shoved him aside gently, hiding his anger. "Take this infant away, Gallahan," he told the hatless skeleton, "and tell him the facts of life."

Gallahan guffawed. "He's a journalist, Wentworth," he said. "Just out of Columbia. But you better give us something to shut up the desk. Otherwise they'll keep us camping on your door-step all night."

Wentworth hesitated. What Gallahan said was true. The news men were all friendly to him. He had met them a dozen times in his work as an amateur criminologist under his real name and when he visited his friend, Kirkpatrick, at headquarters. But they would have to stick until they got something that would pass as a statement.

"All right," he said, with resignation and grinned as the young journalist drew out a notebook and a pencil. None of the other newspaper men had even a piece of paper in their hands. They depended upon their trained memories and only jotted down a few important facts, usually after the interview was over. "All right, I've got just this to say: the Avenger is no Robin Hood. He has pocketed at least ten times as much loot as he has given to the poor. As to his charges, they aren't new. I've been accused before this of being the Spider because our trails crossed in working on the same cases. Your files will verify the exonerations."

He turned to find Jenkyns holding the door open. His ruddy old face worried beneath the crown of his silvery hair.

"But, Mr. Wentworth," the youngster crowded forward again, "that's no answer. Are you the Spider?"

Gallahan caught the youngster by the collar and pulled him away struggling.

"Want to answer that one, Wentworth?" he asked quietly.

"The answer is yes, of course," Wentworth said with a smile. "I'm also the Avenger in disguise and that long missing gentleman, Judge Crater. If you dig into my past, you will find suspicious indications also that I am the Lindbergh baby...."

CHAPTER 7
DEATH'S PROFIT

HE CLOSED the door on the guffaws of Gallahan and peered sharply into Jenkyns' face. The old butler was very portly and dignified in his satin knee breeches, but his eyes were tortured. Wentworth surrendered his cape and broad-brimmed hat with a significant glance that told Jenkyns to dispose of them quickly.

"Mr. Kirkpatrick is awaiting you, sir," Jenkyns said impassively. "He has brought Ram Singh home. Wounded, sir."

With a startled exclamation, Wentworth strode into his living room, batting aside the portières with a sweep of his arm. Ram Singh struggled to his feet from a davenport and stood, swaying weakly, a white bandage about his throat.

"Be thou seated, O my wounded warrior," Wentworth told him in Hindustani, and strode across to clasp the hand of his friend, Stanley Kirkpatrick, commissioner of police.

"This was kind of you, Kirk," he said. "Bringing my boy home."

Kirkpatrick looked quizzically into his eyes. "That was not my sole purpose in coming, Dick," he said.

Wentworth lifted his eyebrows in surprise, but his masked gaze studied the saturnine countenance of his friend. Inwardly all was turmoil again. All his fears and tension returned. First, he had been struck with disappointment that Ram Singh had lost the trail when he had hoped to close with the Avenger. Apprehension for his Hindu boy was assuaged now, but the new menace in Kirkpatrick's voice and words shook him anew.

Yet he did not believe his friend had come to arrest him. Wentworth could not picture Kirkpatrick coming to perform that task yet delaying, before he left his office, to attach a gardenia in his lapel as he had. The man was groomed with his usual meticulous perfection, black mustaches waxed to needle points. The perfecto was held so steadily between his lean fingers that the pale blue thread of smoke from it rose straight and unagitated. But Kirkpatrick's blue eyes were shrewd beneath his level brows and there was a light in them that Wentworth could not quite interpret. Wentworth nodded, perfect amiability masking his inward questioning of Kirkpatrick's visit.

"If you will have a seat, Kirk, until I can make sure that Ram Singh is comfortable, I'll be with you. Jenkyns has already found your favorite Scotch for you, I see."

He crossed to Ram Singh and bent solicitously over his shoulder, asking a quiet question in English. His mind scarcely attended Ram Singh's reply in the same language. He still worried over Kirkpatrick's visit. But each thing in it's time. He must listen to Ram Singh.

"I followed a Hooded One I believed to be this man who calls himself the Avenger," said the Hindu in his harsh, slightly nasal voice. "He went into the City Morgue and when he came out, he walked directly to my car. Evidently, he had seen I followed him. Before I had any warning of his intention, he smashed the window of the car with the hilt of a knife and struck at my throat. I had the engine running and jerked into gear at that instant so that his blade grazed, instead of piercing my throat. When I got from the car to attack, he had fled."

"It is considerably more than a graze, Dick," Kirkpatrick interjected in his dry way. "A half-inch to the left and you would be minus a valuable assistant. Luckily the jugular was not ruptured."

"Rest, O Ram Singh," said Wentworth formally. "Tomorrow there is much for us to do."

RAM SINGH got weakly to his feet. He had lost much blood. But Wentworth offered no assistance, knowing that the doughty Sikh would consider a helping hand little short of an insult. The Hindu held his turbaned head proudly as he stalked from the room. Wentworth shook his head slowly, turned to Kirkpatrick with a smile that masked his concern over the commissioner's visit.

"I don't know what I ever did to deserve such faithful men," he said, "but my score with the Avenger is over-heavy now. He shot Jackson. Now he knifes Ram Singh. Furthermore, I believe him to be connected with the forty-seven poisoning deaths of the last two weeks and with the disfigurement of seventeen women tonight."

Kirkpatrick's alert eyes narrowed, his brows lifted. "Any evidence?"

"Not a scintilla," Wentworth admitted.

Kirkpatrick said grimly, "I should like to get evidence against someone in those deaths. They number ninety-seven now and two hundred and four women are in the hospitals with acid burns on their faces."

A startled oath ripped from Wentworth. Truly the criminals, whoever they were, struck with fearful and remorseless efficiency. Two hundred women ruined for life, nearly a hundred human beings slaughtered, and all for no apparent reason.

"By God," he swore, "these crimes must be stopped!"

There was fierce agreement on Kirkpatrick's face, but the quizzical gleam remained in his eyes. "It may be that the Avenger is behind it," he said slowly. "Certainly he does not hesitate to attack anyone. He has gone after the Spider, now."

Wentworth, feeling again the surge of anger that he had known on first learning of the horror the criminals had wrought, glimpsed sardonic amusement in Kirkpatrick's eye. Kirkpatrick knew beyond question that Wentworth was the Spider and had told him so to his face, but there never had been any final proof of that fact. Furthermore, Kirkpatrick admired and respected this killer of the night who struck swiftly and surely where the law's machinery, for all Kirkpatrick's brilliance, could move with only cautious tread. And he had declared an armed truce with Wentworth.

When he could, he would help the Spider in his battles against the underworld, but if ever there came a time when proof was put into his hands—such as that automatic which now the Avenger held—he would act with the full power and brilliance of which he was capable, even if that meant sending his closest friend to the electric chair.

That was why amusement brushed his eyes now, for necessarily these two always referred to the Spider in the third person, as if he were another entity; as if no peril lurked over Wentworth's head; as if that fact could never terribly split their friendship into bloody warfare.

Wentworth met his amusement with a swift question, a polite interest. His heart was drumming. He had been right then, in supposing that Kirkpatrick's visit had to do with the Spider!

"The Avenger delivered into police hands tonight," Kirkpatrick began slowly, answering Wentworth's question, "a damning piece of evidence against the Spider."

Wentworth felt rigidity creep into his poise. Good God! Had he been wrong in his deductions? Had the Avenger after all given Kirkpatrick the automatic? He fought the rigidity, compelled his facial muscles to maintain that air of polite interest. He could not look away. He must keep his eyes on Kirkpatrick's.

"However," the commissioner drawled, "the evidence is not so helpful as it might be. It is a motion picture of the Spider killing that gambler, Mannley. Unfortunately, the Spider wore his usual mask."

WENTWORTH DREW a deep, slow breath as Kirkpatrick pulled his eyes away and turned toward the davenport where he picked up a brief case. It was bad, this latest blow of the Avenger, but it was not as damaging as he had feared. He had been careful to cover all identifying details. His eyes jerked abruptly to Kirkpatrick's compact, assured body as he caught a glint of metal and saw him extract an automatic pistol from the brief case. Some new evidence? But Wentworth was beyond further shocks now. The evening had been nerve-racking. Any new blow would be anti-climactic. Surely, the Great Playwright must see that! No more tonight.

There was a dullness in Wentworth's eyes, a slackness that extended throughout his body as he saw Kirkpatrick turn with the automatic.

"The bullets from this gun did not match with that from Mannley's body," said the Commissioner and held out the gun.

Wentworth reached out his hand carelessly for it, but Kirkpatrick did not release it. His fingers tightened on the barrel which he held. Wentworth felt a numbing coldness in his brain. Good Lord! Some new issue to face? He forced a mild surprise into the lifting of his eyebrows, drove himself to meet his friend's shrewd, blue eyes.

"But," said Kirkpatrick softly. "I do not see why you found it necessary to rout the numbers off your gun."

Wentworth's heart gave a violent thump, then beat hard and slowly in his chest. For a moment he had believed police had discovered that the weapon bore other numbers than his own. But this was just as bad. It was a criminal offense to remove the registered numbers from a fire-arm. He twisted his forehead into a puzzled frown as the automatic came free in his hand. He twisted it up to stare where the number should have been as if he could not quite believe the statement.

"Not just filed off, Dick," Kirkpatrick went on softly, "but routed out. That is a criminal's trick. As long as they are only filed off, certain acid treatments can restore the destroyed numbers by revealing the impression the die made in the basic steel fibers.

Criminals have got hold of that fact and used a router which not only removes the number, but twists the steel fibers beneath so that not even the acids can restore the number. That is what has been done on this automatic."

Wentworth slipped a jeweler's loupe from a table drawer, and studied the surface of the gun closely with the glass screwed into his eye. He felt a mild sense of surprise that his hand did not tremble. Lord, what was the way out of this tangle? He doubted that Kirkpatrick would press charges on account of the routing, but it was a bad spot, especially if his own weapon should turn up later. Suppose the Avenger was keeping it to plant beside some murdered man to doubly damn him! He must disown this weapon. There was no other way.

"This is not my gun," he said slowly.

"It is the gun you gave Trowbridge as your own," Kirkpatrick replied sharply.

WENTWORTH NODDED. "If you recall," he said, "The Avenger and I struggled in Mannley's room. My weapon was knocked from my hand and naturally I supposed when I picked this one up from the floor that it was mine. It is the same make and caliber and I did not examine it closely at the time."

"Then this is the Avenger's weapon?"

Wentworth shrugged. "I have no way of telling. As you say, it is obviously a criminal's weapon."

The two men stood facing each other, both frowning, their eyes masking true thoughts. The mouths of both were set and grim.

"I cannot doubt you speak the truth, Dick," said Kirkpatrick slowly. "I have never known you to lie to me even when the truth might incriminate you. But I must point out that if this is not your gun, then the test of the bullet can not clear you of the Avenger's charges."

Wentworth had expected that, but it was a type of charge he was prepared to meet. He seemed to become a half-inch taller as he drew himself up. His shoulders were braced stiffly, and his gray blue eyes were cold.

"I was not aware," he said stiffly, "that the Avenger's charges were to be taken seriously. Do you wish to put me under arrest?"

Kirkpatrick stared his friend directly in the eyes and slowly the straightened corners of his mouth relaxed.

"No, Dick," he said, a little wearily, "I do not wish to put you under arrest. I am just pointing out a fact to you, a fact that can be very dangerous. I don't know whether the Avenger took your gun or whether your gun fired the bullet that killed Mannley. But you are fighting the Avenger, that I know, and your gun in his hands is a peril to you. Dick, for God's sake, why don't you give up this dangerous life?"

Wentworth allowed himself to relax slightly. He crossed to the table where decanter and soda stood, poured Scotch into a glass and squirted soda into it. He needed a moment to steady himself before he turned slowly to face Kirkpatrick again. This was dangerous ground he was treading.

"Sooner or later, Dick," Kirkpatrick said seriously, "you are bound to make a mistake. Evidence that you are the Spider will fall into my hands and you know that, even if afterward I killed myself for it, I would use that evidence as it should be employed. You seem to bear a charmed life where the bullets of your enemies are concerned. But it can't go on. Not forever!"

Earnestly, Kirkpatrick stepped toward Wentworth, placed a hand on either shoulder. For once Wentworth did not meet his eyes, kept his gaze on the pale amber liquor that he sloshed thoughtfully about in his glass. He knew in what deep affection the Commissioner held him and he reciprocated it fully. Sometimes, it was good sport to match wits with him, but there had been times—as now—when it was not so pleasant. Times when it seemed inevitable that they must meet in life or death struggle.

If he did not meet Kirkpatrick's gaze, it was not because he could not. It was because he feared that the pain he felt at this meeting might be too plainly there, the pain that he could not answer his friend straightforwardly.

"I don't ask you to consider me, Dick," Kirkpatrick went on and his fingers ate deep into Wentworth's shoulders. "Men are men and can take the blows as they come. But, Dick… think of Nita. Think what your downfall would cost her. She would bear it proudly, because it is her blood and her heritage. But it would kill her, Dick, as surely as if the bullet that brought you down, the electric current in the chair, passed through her own body."

Wentworth was rigid under his grip now. The glass was clenched tightly in his hand, so tightly that it quivered slightly. Kirkpatrick was silent for a moment. When he spoke again, his voice was rasping and harsh.

"For God's sake, Dick, quit before it is too late. I feel… I feel that the end is near. I feel it here." He dropped his hands from

Wentworth's shoulders and pounded a doubled fist against his chest.

A QUIVER ran through Wentworth. He was not superstitious, but he was a fatalist. He believed that in every man's life, the days were numbered. He believed that he, too, someday would come face to face with that day. When his muscles would falter in a crisis, when his bullet would not speed true; when his over-wearied brain would make a mistake he could not rectify. For a moment the picture that Kirkpatrick had conjured up flicked through his mind. Nita, with him dead in the electric chair or bowled over by a gangster's bullet....

There was a sharp, tinkling crash and Wentworth looked down at his hand and saw that the glass had crushed in his grip. There was a tiny red gash of red across his fingers, an irregular damp splotch upon the golden pile of the carpet.

"Careless of me," he muttered.

The mask dropped over his face. He could not permit himself these thoughts. He drove the quiver of apprehension from his body, the sick thoughts from his mind, looked up with a quick smile.

"You know," he said, "I would have sworn it was impossible for a man to crush a glass in his hand. It must have been cracked."

Kirkpatrick stared at him with eyes that had grown haggard. His face seemed suddenly drawn and old. His head shook slowly; he sucked in a deep breath, then moved his shoulders wearily as though he adjusted them to an ancient and heavy burden.

"I knew it wouldn't do any good, Dick," he said dully. "But I had to try. I'm telling you the truth." Once more he struck his clenched fist against his chest. "I feel it here. This is the end!"

Wentworth's heart went out to his friend, but there was nothing he could do, nothing he could say. Even his expression of understanding would put an additional burden upon his friend, a bit of evidence against the Spider that he must ignore. And he could not turn from the path to which he had set his feet. Until the bitter end, he would drive on for the salvation of humanity, fight for the people against the encroachment of the underworld. When the end came—

He smiled slowly, a grimace that was stiff upon his otherwise expressionless face.

"Jenkyns," he raised his voice. "Bring another glass. And bring Mr. Kirkpatrick a gardenia."

Kirkpatrick looked slowly down to his lapel. The flower was crushed.

CHAPTER 8
THE MURDERS GO ON

THE TWO men stood silently while Jenkyns came and went. When Kirkpatrick spoke again, it was as if he had never brought up the subject of the Spider.

"Have you any idea of who the Avenger might be?" he asked quietly.

Wentworth made a grimace, told Kirkpatrick of the three men he had seen at Mannley's who might fit the description, Commander Samuels, the croupier Larue with his green eye-shade, and Deputy Marshant. Kirkpatrick jerked a hand impatiently.

"They're all out of the question," he said irritably. "How about young Shane Malone?"

Wentworth shook his head decidedly. "Just a kid, and besides I saw him and the Avenger side by side."

"But Ram Singh saw two men in the Avenger's disguise," Kirkpatrick pointed out. "That might easily have been framed as an alibi for Malone if the need arose."

Wentworth laughed, but the sound was a little shaky—emotion had left its mark. He crossed to the taborette to mix himself another drink. "Your guess is as good as mine," he said. "There is no clue except the Russian accent, and that might easily be assumed. The Avenger told the newspapers he was a famous detective, which probably means that he isn't. I suggest that we check on the movements of these men I have mentioned and see first whether they have alibis. But I'll admit that if any one of them had alibis for all the occasions, it would be more suspicious than otherwise."

Kirkpatrick brushed the whole matter aside, his saturnine face gone grave.

"Frankly, I am less interested in the Avenger's forays than in these poison murders," he said, his words clipped and brittle. "You have a hunch the two are connected, but that scarcely justifies our hunting for only one man."

Wentworth agreed with that. It was the decision he had reached himself. Despite the threat of the automatic that the

Avenger held, he determined to throw all his energies into a quest for the criminals behind the poison and acid attacks….

The next day found the death-toll mounting steadily and only when Kirkpatrick enforced a rigid embargo on the sale of both canned meat and cosmetics did the hospital reports dwindle.

Death broke out also in neighboring cities, in New Jersey, and even as far upstate as Albany. By night of the second day, two thousand were dead and the women whose faces were destroyed were nearly triple that number!

The canned meat company, to which the poison had been traced, was indicted for criminal negligence as was the cosmetic firm. Both were deluged with damage suits and bankruptcy was inevitable.

Wentworth was not permitted to forget the Avenger. Eddie Blanton and the other four newspaper men had been only an advance guard, for day and night, his doors were besieged by reporters. The Avenger had reinforced his charges against Wentworth by publicizing the motion picture film he had sent to police. Huge full-length pictures from it were printed by newspapers and showed the Spider killing the gambler, Mannley; showed him printing his seal upon the ace of spades.

One newspaper was running a series of full-page articles called: "Who is the Spider?" These detailed every battle which the Spider had fought with the underworld. They gave police records of the number of times Richard Wentworth had been put under arrest on charges that identified him with the Spider—and they printed in just as great detail, his exonerations. The *Press*, for which Eddie Blanton worked, was offering a ten-thousand-dollar reward for evidence that would convict anyone of being the Spider.

Added to the fifty thousand dollars which already had been placed upon the Spider's head, it made a small fortune. An army of amateur and private detectives camped upon Wentworth's trail, since the newspapers pointed out that absolute proof would be necessary.

IT WAS the day on which Jackson came home from the hospital that Wentworth learned through a news flash that the Avenger had struck in Chicago; he wounded two men and left two others helpless prisoners beside the looted safe of a large jewelry concern. It was unfortunate, the Avenger phoned the newspapers, that he had been unable to save the loot.

Nita was with Wentworth a few hours later when the newspapers reported that the Avenger had struck again, that he had deposited near police headquarters the body of a gangster who, the Avenger said, had slain a witness to a killing. The gangster was one of the chief aids of the dead gang leader, O'Burke, a man who might logically have succeeded to his scepter. It was the Avenger's first kill and Wentworth smiled thinly over the entry and summoned Ram Singh and Jackson to him.

"I shall fly to Chicago tomorrow," he told his faithful servants, keen eyes studying both. "After these victories of the Avenger, I expect that the poisoners will be busy in Chicago tomorrow and I wish to be there to investigate. I leave to you the running down of such clues as we have here.

"Ram Singh, look over all of Mannley's associates. There must have been a connection between him and the Avenger."

The Hindu bowed, sweeping his cupped bands to his turbaned forehead.

"Han, sahib," his nasal voice was strong.

"I want you also to check up on three men: Commander Samuels; the croupier at Mannley's who is built like the Avenger and wears a green eye-shade; and Mr. Kirkpatrick's deputy, Marshant."

"Han, sahib," Ram Singh repeated. He turned and strode from the room.

"Jackson," Wentworth said his eyes boring into the clear blue gaze of his ex-sergeant. "I want you to investigate Patsy Malone."

Jackson's expression did not change, his eyes did not waver, but Wentworth thought he detected a tensing of the prominent muscles along his wide jaws, a heritage from some Gascon forebear.

"I am not ready," Wentworth continued gravely, "to accuse her of deliberately assisting a plot against me. Her behavior at the time I invaded her apartment might well have been gratitude for the Avenger returning that forged check to her brother. But I do believe that the Avenger used her and her brother to set a trap for me."

"If the Major pleases," Jackson interrupted, his voice wooden, "might it not have been possible for this crook, Mannley, to trap Shane, then have a man of his get nasty to Pat—to Miss Malone—in the restaurant where they knew I ate?"

Wentworth nodded slowly, his eyes serious as he studied Jackson's loyal face.

"Yes, that would have been easily possible," he agreed. "I want you to discover that man's identity and learn whatever else is possible about the connection between Patsy Malone and the Avenger.

"I have prepared to disappear from sight and completely wipe out my identity as Wentworth if the Avenger acts against me," he added slowly. "But it is a step for dire emergency only. It would hamper me terrifically in my work. I want to locate the man and clip his claws first. I know I am asking a great deal of you, Jackson, to ask that you investigate a girl in whom you evidently are deeply interested, but it is for that very reason that I assign you to the task."

Jackson's brows tightened down over his eyes. "The Major asks nothing. If I hadn't horned in and got myself shot...."

"We won't mention that angle of it, Jackson," Wentworth said kindly. "Just push on with the investigation and learn what you can. Also, I will arrange a Spider disguise for you. I want you to show yourself in it once or twice while I am in Chicago to mislead police and the Avenger and so to give me a possible alibi."

Jackson saluted, about-faced and stalked from the room with his shoulders set stiffly. His wound had begun to heal and would not hinder him in his work, provided he did not tangle in a rough-and-ready fight with the criminals. When Jackson had gone, Wentworth turned to Nita and found a faint smile upon her lips.

"Jackson loves that girl," she said softly.

Wentworth nodded agreement. "But he is loyal to me," he

pointed out, "and because the girl must know his affections are involved, I think she will be truthful with him."

NITA OBVIOUSLY was not thinking of Jackson and the girl. Her eyes were intent under lowered lids. Her head was thrown back against the wine-red of the velvet-covered davenport and a shaded lamp made bronze lights among her curls.

"Is what you told Jackson true, Dick," she asked gently. "Are you prepared to disappear entirely?"

"Yes," Wentworth told her. "You are thinking that it was perhaps unwise to tell a man of divided loyalties my plans?"

"That, yes," Nita agreed, "and also—" she hesitated, lifting her head and looking down at a cigarette she tapped absently against a case, "and also you hadn't told me your plans."

Wentworth did not smile as he stepped swiftly forward and snapped flame to Nita's cigarette. "I'm not going to tell you, sweetheart, either," he said quietly. "If I disappear, it will be because Kirkpatrick has in his hands evidence that will convict me of being the Spider. You wouldn't expect me to involve you in any such mess as that would you?"

Nita rose slowly to her feet, tossing the cigarette into a tray. "But if I insist on being involved?" Her red lips were curved invitingly, but her eyes were deadly serious.

Wentworth caught her close in his arms. His mouth shut grimly. Nita leaned backward in his arms, hands upon his shoulders, eyes gazing steadily into his. Wentworth's stiff lips twisted into the mockery of a smile. "I cannot, dear," he told her. "I refuse to involve you."

And though Nita first coaxed, then grew angry, he would not

reveal his plans. She smiled wanly as she prepared to leave, then suddenly flung herself into his arms.

"Oh, Dick," she gasped. "For both our sakes, be careful!"

His answer was a kiss and Nita left pushing her way disdainfully through a group of questioning newspaper men who waited always outside his door.

Wentworth prepared swiftly to leave the city. He packed no clothing, carried no luggage. He merely picked up a cane, shrugged into his dark overcoat and stalked out of his apartment a few minutes behind Nita.

The reporter, Eddie Blanton, was immediately at his side, a grin on his horsey face. "Going out to make a kill, Spider!" he jibed.

Wentworth nodded gravely. "Yes, I've decided your city editor must answer for his sins. He abuses his men."

Blanton swept a bow so low that he threatened to pitch forward on his face. "I shall be your eternal debtor," he swore.

The other newspaper men watched narrowly, piled into the elevator behind Wentworth. He stalked through the lobby with the entire straggling crowd on his heels. Outside the door of his building, a group of people stood. Bedraggled boys, dirty faced and scantily clothed, pointing their fingers.

"There goes the Spider!" one yelled shrilly.

Men stared at him with speculative eyes from behind the line police had set up, for Wentworth had been compelled to ask Kirkpatrick for a guard against the mobs that newspaper publicity had set upon his heels.

Among the watching crowd were women also. They seemed

strangely pale and for a moment that fact puzzled Wentworth. He stared again and found that fear made their countenances haggard, but more than that, not one of them used cosmetics. Powder and rouge and lipstick had been abandoned since acid burns had forced hundreds of women to go through life with faces scarred and welted and disfigured.

THE DISCOVERY struck Wentworth with the sharp pain of a knife wound. His lips tightened. Something must be done at once to relieve the terror of these people. But how could he act, hampered as he was? Everywhere he went the newspaper men followed. His picture had been smeared over the pages of every newspaper in the city and on the streets, crowds turned to stare at him and urchins pointed, grimy fingers. Worse than that, there were dozens of amateur detectives always upon his trail, seeking a share in that sixty-thousand reward.

At the curb, Wentworth signaled a taxi and cursed as he saw recognition even in the driver's eyes. Damn it, he must elude this constant surveillance! The cab buzzed swiftly up Fifth Avenue. Wentworth could find only one cab that seemed to be following and that dropped off before he had covered five blocks. Wentworth frowned heavily. It was probable that Blanton had signaled some other newspaper man, one Wentworth did not know by sight, to take up the trail.

He sent his taxi on a zigzag course until he spotted the cab that trailed him, then he alighted and walked directly toward the machine, climbed in while the passenger looked at him with frightened eyes.

"As long as we're going the same way," Wentworth said. "I may as well save you taxi fare."

The man forced a smile to his lips. "You understand how it is, Mr. Wentworth," he said. "I've got a job to do…."

Wentworth said, "Sure, you have a job to do."

The cab driver was staring back at them, a frown of painful thought wrinkling his face like a monkey's. "Newark airport," Wentworth commanded.

At the airport, three quarters of an hour later, Wentworth, politely but firmly refusing to permit the newspaper man to phone his office, bought two tickets for Washington and ushered his prisoner onto the plane. When the co-pilot swung aboard with his passenger list fluttering on a clip board, Wentworth walked excitedly to the door.

"This isn't the plane for Pittsburgh," he said violently. "Let me off of here!"

He thrust the astonished co-pilot aside, climbed to the ground. "I should think you'd keep intelligent attendants around here," he continued angrily. "Telling me this was the Pittsburgh plane!"

The co-pilot apologized and shut the door. The plane took off with the newspaper man aboard, gently sleeping. In about an hour he would recover from the narcotic Wentworth had needled into his veins. By that time the plane would be past Philadelphia and sweeping on toward Baltimore… and Wentworth would be well on his way to Chicago.

DAWN WAS gray in the east and the yellow sprinkling of lights that dusted over Chicago proper was dwindling when

Wentworth's plane set down on the field there. He went directly to a hotel and once in his room, flung himself down to sleep. At noon he arose, had lunch and made some purchases. The afternoon papers made no mention of the poisonings he expected, but he was still sure they impended.

In his room, he took his stand before a mirror and went to work on his disguise. He affixed to his upper lip a mustache that followed the line of his mouth and extended below its corners, giving his whole face a slightly discouraged droop. He made his cheeks puffed and ruddy, then oiled his hair and brushed it straight back from his forehead. He grayed the temples and finally donned thick-lensed glasses. He put on a suit of Scotch tweeds, topcoat and a crushed slouch hat, then swaggered out of the hotel with pigskin gloves and a cane in his fist. He walked with a quick, choppy step, tapping the cane briskly, beaming from behind his thick glasses, a smile upon his lips that were thick and much too red. But the smile was forced. Here, too, the women had pale, haunted faces, bare of cosmetics. It seemed to him the men, too, moved with a furtive, frightened air.

Wentworth turned back to his swift, choppy pacing, and a block further on, entered police headquarters. They accepted him and his forged police-card at face value. Carl Southers, it said, of the New York Press had arrived to do a story on the Avenger in Chicago. He was in the station press-room, making himself pleasant to the half-envious, half-sneering newspaper men of Chicago, when the reports of fresh poisonings began to tap into headquarters with the regularity of drum-beats.

A family of five had been stricken in South Chicago. These

were Negroes and three had died before they reached the hospital, the other two soon afterward. A relay from nearby Cicero reported two men and a woman had collapsed in a restaurant. In each case, the victims had dined on canned salmon. Wentworth watched these reports with mounting rage. They confirmed his theories about the Avenger, but it was horrible to sit helplessly while human beings died.

Wentworth took a taxi directly to the restaurant where the last attack had been reported and found that police had closed the place. The cop at the door fended Wentworth off, only grunting at his press-card, and Wentworth paced briskly away with his assumed choppy stride, tapping his cane. He circled the block, entered the alley back of the restaurant. He fished a salmon tin from the restaurant's garbage can. He made a note of the brand and the manufacturer, then paced away again.

When he got back to headquarters there had been fifty-seven more deaths from poison and in each case the victims had eaten salmon.

The deaths were mounting and still the reason for the attack was not apparent. His guess that an outbreak was due in Chicago, based on the fact that the Avenger had shifted his operations to the city, had been confirmed. But he was still as far as ever from discovering motive and methods. And meantime, the slaughter went on.

At the hotel, he went directly to his room—he had retained the key—and found a man leaning against the door with an expression of weary patience on his face. As Wentworth came into sight, the man swayed his weight away from the wall and blinked at him with shrewd, amused eyes.

It was Eddie Blanton. "Howdy, Mr. Wentworth!" he said, grinning.

CHAPTER 9
A CLUE—AND DEATH!

B LANTON BROKE off with a low curse of amazement as Wentworth, opening the door, allowed the light from his room to stream over him.

"That's a damned clever get-up," the reporter said. "You're a dead ringer for one of the boys on the paper. In fact, if I hadn't taken a tip from you and used disguise, come all the way here with you in the same plane, I'd think I'd made a mistake."

Wentworth felt a sinking sensation within him. He had thought himself safe from surveillance for a while. It had been a relief to walk the streets without seeing startled, half-frightened recognition on the faces he passed. Now Blanton had arisen to harass and hamper him. But Wentworth's face showed only annoyance.

"You must excuse me," he said with stiff boorishness, "if I seem inhospitable, but despite your familiar manners, I have no idea what you are talking about."

He entered the room and shut the door, hearing Blanton curse through the panels, and stood staring blankly across the room, hat and coat still on, cane gripped in his hand. He did not for a moment think that his attitude had fooled Blanton. But the fact that the reporter had followed him was a severe handicap. Apparently the newspaper man was keeping a detailed check of his movements and the fact that Wentworth and the Spider made a simultaneous appearance in a city would make a nice story for the Press.

Furthermore, the Avenger held evidence that would convict him. Indeed, he might already have turned it over to the police in New York. A feeling of panic, new to his years of battling against unbelievable odds, rippled over Wentworth. He found his muscles tense, found himself listening acutely for the approach of the law's myrmidons. The only sound was Blanton's weary knocking at the door.

WENTWORTH EVADED Blanton by summoning a hotel porter to his room to remove a trunk, bribing the man and walking out in his clothing, face disguised. Blanton trotted after him but Wentworth grinned and would not talk and Blanton went back to the hotel room door to watch.

Wentworth spent the night and all the next day making a list of the firms competing with the handlers of Gold Moon salmon and with the companies which were being driven into bankruptcy by the poison in canned corn beef and the acid in cosmetics.

On the third day after his arrival in Chicago, as he prepared to begin the final phase of his work there, a phone call from Nita brought him disquieting news.

"Jackson was almost arrested last night, dear," she reported in a voice she tried vainly to keep unfrightened and calm. "He was out in that Spider disguise, wearing the steel mask you prepared for him, and some one saw him and called police. He was surrounded and, in escaping, his mask was torn off. They recognized him as your chauffeur. The newspapers are going crazy with it."

Wentworth went slowly back to work on the disguise, still frowning. His jaw was set grimly as he finished making up his face and left his rooms to begin a rounds of the companies.

Then Wentworth put the matter out of his head for the time being while he followed down the details of his new theory of the poisoning. In each office of companies that distributed canned salmon, he forced his way into the presence of the firm's active head and asked questions.

Had anyone attempted to obtain money from them under threats?

Had anyone offered them an inspection service as a guarantee against poisonings?

Have they been offered insurance against poisonings?

Had they ever had any dealings with racketeers?

IN EVERY case, Wentworth met only denials, but in fully half the places he visited, he read fear and evasion in the faces of the officials. The pale, unrouged cheeks of office girls goaded him on. Finally, entering the offices of the Silver Sea salmon company, he saw that he had been preceded by a lean six-footer who rolled his shoulders in a brown camel's-hair coat. The man had a lowering, dark face beneath the turned-down brim of a brown felt and he scowled with feeling when he saw Wentworth.

For Wentworth's disguise screamed that he was policeman, from his broad-toed shoes to his brown derby, from his swagger

manner of unaccustomed authority to the piercing suspicious gaze of his eyes. And Wentworth recognized the man, a private detective named Nettleton whom he had once employed. He felt his heart leap with hope. If the company was calling in a

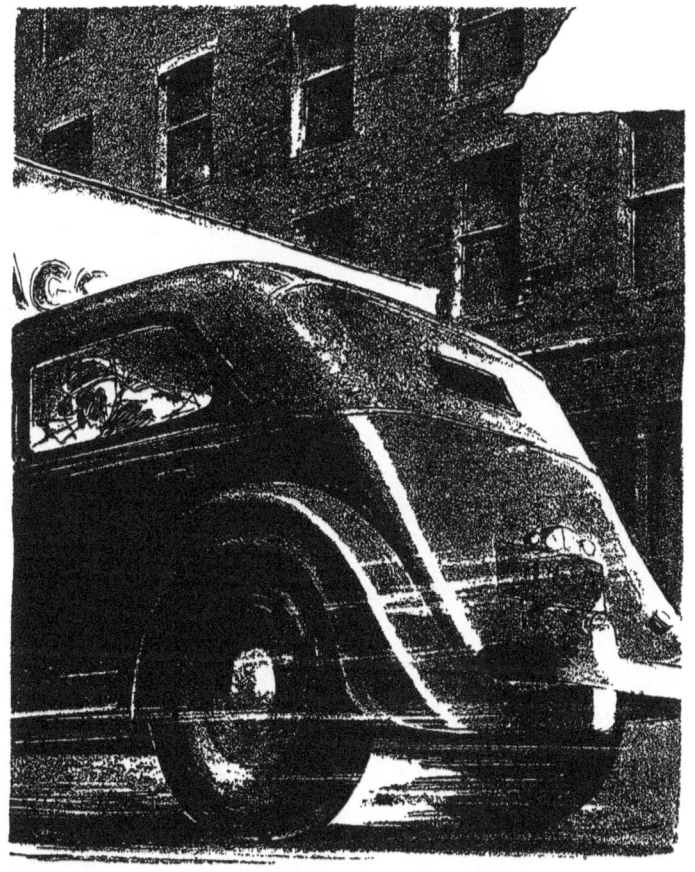

The shriek became a scream; then a crashing slam that mingled with the shouts of men!

private detective, it more than half-confirmed his theories. A firm might fear to inform the police, yet use private agencies.

When the man in the camel's-hair coat scowled at him and

jerked his broad shoulders angrily in passing, Wentworth turned and walked out behind him.

"Just a minute," he growled.

The man in the long coat spun about and came at him on pounding feet, jabbing a rigid forefinger against his breastbone.

"Listen, dick," he said sharply. "I've got enough of being ridden by headquarters, see. Just lay off." He spun on his heel.

"I said wait a minute!" Wentworth snapped. He went, heavily heeled, down the hall behind Nettleton.

The detective swung about and his neck was red and swelling with anger.

"I told you I had enough of it," he said in a slow, thick voice. "First off, you frame my partner for blackmail, then you frisk my office, and now you start shadowing me. I'm sick of it, and...."

Wentworth listened to the tirade with his brows knitted, his eyes peering up sharply from under bushy eyebrows. It was apparent the cops had been riding this fellow and he probably had it coming to him. He was hard-boiled and not over-scrupulous. But that wasn't going to help Wentworth any in getting information. It was probable that Nettleton had been called in by this firm partly because of his known hostility toward police. He crowded up close to Nettleton and jabbed the muzzle of his automatic against the hard muscle plates of his belly.

"You're coming with me," he said shortly. Nettleton quit talking in the middle of a word and his mouth stayed open. Wentworth whirled him with a punch at his shoulder, slapped over his pockets and took out two guns. Then he herded Nettleton ahead of him out of the building.

"What the hell is this?" the detective demanded furiously.

"It isn't a pinch," Wentworth told him and volunteered nothing else.

He jabbed the man into a coupé he had rented, handcuffed him to the steering post before he, too, climbed in. Nettleton's eyes were small black beads that glittered through lid-crowded slits. Wentworth shoved the car downwind between high factory walls and ignored his prisoner. Gradually Nettleton's anger gave way to a half-fearful bewilderment.

He cursed explosively. "You're no dick!"

Wentworth admitted that without hesitation. "I just wanted to talk to you," he explained, "and I wanted you to be in a reasonable frame of mind. I'm willing to pay for information."

Nettleton's eyes were still narrow, but the gleam in them now had to do with cupidity. "What do you want to know?" he growled. "You sure got your nerve with you, strong-arming me this way."

"What did the Silver Sea people want?" Wentworth asked. "I'm willing to pay five thousand for an answer I can believe."

"Go to hell," Nettleton said savagely.

Wentworth smiled quietly. He knew his man and he knew the meaning of that gleam in Nettleton's eye. In the end he got his information—at a price. The firm had called Nettleton because it feared to go to police. The afternoon before, a mild-mannered old professor calling himself Gottstalk had offered an inspection-service as a safeguard against poison getting into their canned goods. He had demanded a hundred thousand a year for the service.

CHAPTER 10
THE GENTLE PROFESSOR

THE PRESIDENT of the company, naturally, had turned him down flat and the man had arisen with a vague smile and said he hoped nothing would happen to poison consumers of Silver Sea salmon. He mentioned that the Golden Moon people had turned down his help.

Nettleton snorted. "It's the old racket in a new dress," he declared. "The old protection racket. In the old days, a man paid or his shop was wrecked. Now they gotta pay or they get wiped out by damage suits and criminal prosecution. Silver Sea wants me to put guards on their plant to keep out poison."

Wentworth heard the story without outward excitement, but inwardly he was burning with his discovery. This was a final confirmation of all that he had speculated. His theory of the explanations behind the poisonings and the use of acids had been purely guesswork, but Nettleton's story confirmed it down to the last detail. Now he was on fire to be rid of the detective and tackle the men behind these murders.

There was a cold certainty within him that he would strike without mercy. Men who could so heartlessly wipe out thousands and mutilate hundreds of women simply to line their pockets deserved not even the break of having a gun in their own hands. They should be shot on sight like the mad dogs that they were. But first he must be rid of Nettleton.

Wentworth pulled the coupé to a halt where a street car line meandered between brick walls, unlocked Nettleton and gave him his guns, empty, plus seven thousand dollars in cash.

WENTWORTH GOT rid of his broad-toed shoes, and the rest of the disguise, purchased new materials and had dinner before he drove a newly rented car toward the residence of Professor Gottstalk, which he had previously scouted.

The car seemed almost to sidle up Michigan Boulevard as it fought the howling wind, then turned and scampered down-wind on a side street. He drew to a halt in the shadows a half-block away, then walked swiftly up the dark street. Houses sat well back, their windows glowing orange through the shrubbery. Trees rattled bare boughs overhead. As he pushed along into the wind, windows began to go dark about him.

He had purposely dallied over his supper, taken time to assemble the articles for disguise and now, halting in the dark shadow of a hedge, he swiftly affixed a mustache he had prepared, twisted his mouth with a false scar and used acid to pucker one eye into a squint. Blond wig and brows completed the swift transformation. Then he hurried on. It was nearing midnight and he wanted to enter by the door of the house, rather than risk an invasion by window. He suspected the racketeers would have thrown many guards about the professor and would be painfully alert on the night after he had made his contacts with the potential victims. It would be much more difficult to enter this isolated house than to force his way into apartment quarters in the city.

Minutes later, he swung from the street up the sidewalk to a large house that sat even farther back from the roadway than most of the mansions along Hamilton Avenue. His footsteps rang sharply. His hands in his overcoat pockets, grasped tear-gas bombs. Under his arms nestled two automatics; a black-jack dangled from each wrist, concealed up his sleeves. What he proposed to do was enter the house openly, overpower any guards that showed themselves and take the professor a prisoner.

Wentworth's lips twitched in a small smile and the scar he had executed upon his cheek twisted it into an evil grimace. An open frontal attack would be the last thing these criminals expected—especially from the Spider.

The lights blazed out on the porch as he mounted wooden steps. Wentworth took his hands out of his pockets and walked directly to the door, rang the bell. It raised a dim, echoing clangor within and for moments afterward there was silence. Then the door swung inward on comparative darkness. The lights from the porch shone on the bright canary of a girl's dress; it glinted on her hair. Wentworth raised his blond brows and let the scar distort his smile of greeting. The girl was Patsy Malone!

Wentworth could scarcely suppress the mocking laughter that rose to his lips. Here was a sharp and instant confirmation of all suspicions of the Avenger. The girl's connection with the Hooded One was well established in his own mind and now he found her in the home of the collection man of the racketeers! Another fact sent angry blood pumping through his veins. Patsy used cosmetics. *She* had nothing to fear.

Her opening of the door upset his plans. He had planned to knock out the guard at the door, follow that up with a swift and

White liquid flew from the receptacle straight at Wentworth's face!

ruthless sweep through the house until he could seize and carry off the professor. But he could not bowl over this girl.

"What do you want?" she asked sharply.

Her small, shapely body was tense with alarm, and there was an artificiality about her voice, a strained, unnatural quality that told Wentworth more plainly than any words that she was not alone. Somewhere in the dim reaches of that hall, Wentworth knew there were guns centering upon him. But there was no change in his manner.

"Howdy, Patsy," he said and stepped forward.

The girl shrank back, and Wentworth was upon her in a bound, left arm sweeping her from her feet and against his breast. His foot kicked back and slammed the door and instantly his hand flicked a gas bomb from his pocket and tossed it back into the hall's shadows. The girl's cry of fright and surprise blended with the muffled blast of the bomb. Wentworth saw its gray vapors rise ghost-like in the half-light, saw two men reeling. They coughed and wheezed frantically, fled into the deeper darkness behind them.

One man came toward him, bounding with long-legged leaps, gun glinting in his hand. Wentworth saw that it was Patsy's brother, Shane. He went toward him with the struggling girl still locked against his breast. One of the blackjacks swung into play and Shane went down and out.

Patsy had knocked off Wentworth's hat and fixed both hands in the hair of the wig. She tugged at this now and it came free in her hands. She gasped and Wentworth set her down, whirled her about so that her arms were behind her and locked them there with the grip of his left hand.

"Take me to the professor, Patsy," he ordered softly. "Little girls ought not to mix in gangster affairs."

The girl was sobbing, striking out with her high heels. "You killed Shane," she gasped. "You... you...!"

Wentworth skillfully dodged her kicks and shoved her toward broad stairs that led upward.

"His skull's too thick to kill that easily," he grunted. "But I'm not sure yours is. Take me to the professor."

FEET WERE pounding along the hall upstairs. Wentworth had heard the two men he had gassed flee out of the back door, but now that door slammed again and more men came in.

"Let me go! Let me go to Shane!" Patsy pleaded. She was writhing, sobbing and fighting and it taxed Wentworth's strength to pinion her with his one hand while he held his automatic ready for the impending attack.

"Tell me where the professor is," Wentworth insisted, "and you can go." He dragged Patsy to the right, to a doorway where the two of them were half-protected by the walls.

"He's upstairs," Patsy panted, "in his laboratory. Now, let me...!"

Wentworth released her and she plunged across the hallway and dropped on her knees beside her brother. Wentworth's scar twisted mouth was grim, but there was a pleased light in his eyes. After all these days of wasted effort, he was at last tangling with the killers. The odds were great, but the Spider was used to facing impossible situations—and winning. He crouched in the hallway and the attacking footsteps above and in the back hall ceased.

The men on the floor with him beat a hurried retreat, coughing and sneezing from the remnants of the gas. Wentworth blinked. The tear fumes were beginning to reach out toward him. He would have to climb those stairs, or….

Behind him, in the darkened room, a man stumbled.

Wentworth flung a second gas bomb violently at the spot and slid out into the hall. At the head of the steps, a gun glinted and the Spider's automatic crashed. The gangster gun bounced against the railing, fell to the steps and from the overhead darkness, a man cursed raggedly. Wentworth flung two more shots at the voice and sprang for the stairs.

In the darkness, the white ghost of a face rose behind the banister and Wentworth flung a fourth shot at it, saw the glimmer of it go backward and heard a body thud to the floor. He whirled at the head of the stairs and a heavy gun boomed below. Lead crunched into the banister by his hand. Wentworth could not wait to answer that. In moments, that gunman would be blinded by tear gas anyway.

He began a hurried canvass of the second floor rooms, yanking their doors open and spraying the diffused beam of a pencil flashlight over them. Four were empty. A gun blasted from the fifth and Wentworth's answering lead wrung a dying scream from the gunman. The Spider flipped his nearly empty gun to his left hand, caught a fully loaded one from his holster with his right and streaked toward the third and top floor.

Directly ahead of him was a wide open door that was blindingly bright. White light blazed from it and through the dazzle, Wentworth could make out the cold glisten of glass tubes in racks, of shelves of bottles: the laboratory! He took the final stairs in a single leap, and went in behind his gun. The figure of a gray man, warped by age, half-straightened from where a retort bubbled on the bench. The man continued to stir a brilliant, blue liquid with a glass rod, but he twisted a scrawny neck about so that his beady eyes, shadowed by thick white brows, peered directly at Wentworth.

"What do you want?" he demanded in a rasping voice.

"You!" Wentworth said softly. "Come on! Get your coat. You're going with me!"

The professor blinked as his gaze dropped to the automatics in Wentworth's hands. It lifted again to his face.

"Who are you?" he demanded. "And why should I go with you?"

Wentworth's acutely attuned ears heard heavy feet pounding the stairs, knew that the gangsters were rushing upward to prevent him from escaping with the professor. He did not answer the old man, but strode to where a long gray cape hung from a peg beneath a black hat. He returned to the professor with the garments.

"I haven't time to argue," he snapped, "but unless you come at once, I'll have to knock you out and carry you."

The professor stood still stirring the retort, his beady eyes glittering. "Just let me finish this experiment," he pleaded and reached for the shelf before him.

His hand grasped a bottle, then moved with incredible speed.

It snapped the glass cover free and a globe of white liquid flew from the receptacle directly at Wentworth's face.

He flung up his arm on guard and the liquid splashed upon it. Flying cold fragments struck his face and an overpowering, sweet scent cloyed his nostrils. Wentworth stopped his breath in the middle of an inhalation, wheeled toward the door. He took two staggering steps and pitched forward on his face, unconscious.

Professor Gottstalk chuckled gustily deep in his throat. "Come and get him, boys," he called. "He can't hurt you now." He chuckled again and kept on stirring the blue liquid with a glass rod.

CHAPTER 11
THE AVENGER'S MERCY

WENTWORTH CAME loggily to his senses. He felt that he was riding in a smoothly moving automobile, riding over city streets, but he did not open his eyes.

A harsh voice at his right side growled: "Ain't this punk ever gonna come out of it?"

A voice from the front of the car—Wentworth judged it was the driver—snarled back: "Slap him some more! Go on! Slap him 'til he comes out of it, like the boss said."

Wentworth felt the man beside him grip his shoulder roughly, felt the fellow's calloused hand slap his face ringingly twice—three times. For a moment he took it, let the other go on striking him. Then he made his eyes flutter open, gagged: "Hey! What the hell?" in a falsely weak voice.

He looked into a square, hard face, looked at a typical gangster type. "O.K.!" the burly man growled. "So you've come around, eh?"

Wentworth choked again, nodded with simulated feebleness. "Yes. What are you going to do with me?"

"Stop the bus, Jake," the gangster called to the man in the front seat. "He's O.K., now." Turning back to Wentworth, the hood pulled out a letter, shoved it into the Spider's hands. "There! The Avenger said to give you this." He opened the door beside him when the car had drawn to a halt. "Now scram, buddy. Get out. On your way."

Wentworth waited no second invitation. He gripped the letter in one hand, scrambled out the open door. The driver made the gears grind, and the auto careened away. Wentworth was standing on the curb in a residential section of the city. He tore open the letter, read the words inside:

WENTWORTH—THE SPIDER:

Next time I won't save you when your foolhardiness gets you into a tight place. But I had to keep Martin from disposing of you, because I'm saving you for later on. Right now I haven't time to see that you're convicted. I have to stop Martin. He plans to poison thousands in the East as a buildup for organizing the patent medicine industries. He plans to poison the cold cures in New York. However, if you'll be kind enough to mention the time and place, after we're both back in New York, I'll meet you on even terms. And when that happens, I'll see that you, Richard Wentworth, are proven conclusively to be the Spider. And so until we meet, dear enemy…

THE AVENGER.

Wentworth was astounded by the calm effrontery of the man. He read the note again; realized how cleverly the Avenger had foiled him. He whistled at a cruising taxi, piled in, shouting: "The airport!" And as he settled back in the imitation leather upholstery, he muttered grimly to himself: "And I'm still not sure that Martin and the Avenger aren't the same person!"

At the airport, hangar doors were tight shut against gusty gray skies, and except for a few mechanics and necessary port officials, there was no one about. All mail and transport planes had been grounded. No word had come from the East for hours. Only crashing static sounded on the wireless when Wentworth tried to establish contact. He finally succeeded in buying a plane. Wentworth smiled thinly at officials, ignored their dire warnings and took off in the face of a gusty wind that spat snow. He whirled, took the wind on his tail, and fled eastward before it.

Snow that had been feathery when he took off turned to bullets in the lash of the wind. The ceiling was right down on the earth and within moments he was ripping through an impenetrable screen of clouds. It was incredibly cold. Mist began to freeze on Wentworth's goggles. He threw a narrow-eyed glance at his wings. Ice was there, too, forming on the leading edge.

Slowly the ice piled up and the plane became loggy and lifted sullenly to the gusts. Finally Wentworth was forced to the realization that he had only a few minutes of flying time left. The earth was covered thickly with snow. An attempt to put the ship down in that would mean a certain crackup when the soft drifts clutched at his landing gear. Wentworth felt despair welling up in him, but he fought it down, raging silently. Damn Kirkpatrick and his premonitions of disaster! He *would* get through!

Peering down through the night that had dropped upon the earth while he fought the skies, Wentworth caught an occasional gleam of yellow light from scattered houses, but they were far apart. Then, stabbing across the white plains, he caught the long blue-white ray of a train's headlight. It was only a glimpse, then a curtain of whipping snow dropped over his plane. But Wentworth yelled aloud in sudden triumph.

He fished his automatic from under his tunic, pumped lead into the plane's gasoline tank until it caught fire, then hurled himself out into space. He snatched out the rip-ring of his parachute, felt the great bell snap his body like a whip. Down he shot, peering through the welter of white. Finally, he spotted the glow of the train's headlight, the plume of sparks that thundered from its stack.

STARING TOWARD it, Wentworth was scarcely aware of the ground, deep in snow, flashing upward. He smacked into a drift that swallowed him completely. He fought furiously out of the parachute and struggled through the soft, enveloping frigidity of the snow that was almost to his armpits. The plane plunged into the snow, but burning gasoline continued to smear crimson across the sky. The train streaked on.

Wentworth shouted despairingly. Like an echo, the train's whistle keened across the white flats. Sparks showered from its drivers as the brakes were thrown on. A gasp of thankfulness rose in Wentworth's throat. He ploughed toward the stopping train.

An hour later, the train crawled into Cleveland. There, Wentworth finally got a code message in wireless through to New York. He could only hope that Kirkpatrick would realize the fierce need for action and get after the poisoners. He hoped so, but there was only one way to make sure—dash on to New York himself.

Planes were coated with ice, even as they stood on the ground here in Cleveland. Officials would not hear of starting a special train eastward. They had no telegraph.

But Wentworth, by kidnapping a locomotive, engineer, and fireman at pistol point and offering them a ten-thousand-dollar bonus, managed to leave Cleveland.

The train went through almost to Buffalo before it stalled in a snow bank and Wentworth foot-slogged on until he found a jumping taxi that took him to an airport. He bought a seaplane and used its boat bottom to wallow a take-off track through the snow.

It was four hours and fifty-two minutes later that Wentworth sloshed the seaplane into the drifting pack ice of the Hudson and whirled into the protection of an unoccupied pier. He leaped stiffly ashore and moored the craft. He gazed toward the glimmering beacons of New York's high towers, cold against the night sky, and he sucked in a deep breath.

"Now," the Spider muttered," the battle begins!"

CHAPTER 12
THE SPIDER IS DOOMED

WENTWORTH STRODE swiftly along the pier's snow-blanketed planks toward the shore. West Street, along the waterfront, was a wide white desert without a track. He floundered across it to where a greasy-fronted diner showed a yellow glow.

Wentworth ordered coffee, then spotted a pay telephone in a booth at the rear. He scuffed through the sawdust on the floor and called police headquarters. Kirkpatrick's answer was sharp, but there was a weary drag in his voice.

"This is Dick, Kirk," Wentworth said rapidly. "I've been trying to reach you for twenty hours. Did you get my warning from Cleveland? The poison gang is going to switch to patent medicines now. Cold cures first. I can't see any way to stop it except to slap an embargo on all patent medicines."

The cold silence at the other end of the wire stopped Wentworth then. He held the receiver to his ear and slowly a frown gathered a vertical pucker between his eyes. It hurt his cold-flayed face. His cheeks were burning and stiff after the cold.

"What's the matter, Kirk?" he demanded roughly.

"I warned you, Dick," Kirkpatrick's voice was more tired than before. "You've been indicted for Mannley's murder—as the Spider. The best thing to do would be to surrender to me here at once."

"I'll talk with you about that in a minute," Wentworth said in a voice that was husky despite his effort at calmness. "Here's what's in the wind,—and here's the motive behind the poisonings." Wentworth swiftly told him of his discoveries in Chicago, interrupted by Kirkpatrick's sharp monosyllables. New York police had never heard of the gang leader, Martin, any more than Wentworth had.

"I'm pretty sure that it's O'Burke's gang under new leadership that's handling the thing," Wentworth continued, "but this man, Martin, is the brain of the outfit and I have no idea who he is."

"O'Burke's tie-up in New York is with the McMurty outfit," Kirkpatrick asserted. There was new life in his tones. "We'll watch them, but if it's racketeering, it's a foregone conclusion that we won't be able to get any convictions unless we can catch some men in the act of spreading the poison. And those will not include the leader. We'll never get him."

"And that means the racket will never stop, eh, Kirk?" Wentworth asked. His voice was soft, but there was a hard, wild light in his eyes. "Do you still advise me to surrender, Kirk?" He slammed the receiver and burst out of the booth. His face was without expression as he sat down to eat, then he caught a gleam in the eyes of the pasty-faced counterman and knew suddenly that he had been recognized—recognized as Richard Wentworth, the Spider. Damn this newspaper publicity! The man was sidling toward the telephone even now to call police and seek his share in that sixty-thousand reward.

WENTWORTH BOLTED from the diner and shoved out into the fierce bite of the wind, turned the corner and ran. Police would come fast in answer to the counterman's call. Good

Lord! Had it come to this, that Wentworth was to be hounded wherever he went? That he dared not appear without disguise? He realized with a start that it was for such situations as this that he had made his preparations for disappearance.

He had a passport in another identity. He had money banked abroad which that identity could claim. But Wentworth knew, even as the thought flashed across his brain, that he had no intention of vanishing. Not while so grave a danger menaced the people of his country.

His breath was pumping noisily. The cold was a sharp pain in his cheeks and in his panting lungs. His feet skidded and slipped in the snow. A Ford roadster, whirling dark around a corner ahead, skated into a snow drift, rocked and darted toward him. Wentworth flung flat down in the snow. It had not been cleared here, and well over two feet deep, it covered him entirely. He had no doubt as to the identity of that roadster. It was a police radio patrol car, running dark and silently to seize the Spider.

He heard the muffled roar of its engine as it wallowed through the snow. Had he been spotted before he flung himself flat? Would the policemen spot the abrupt termination of the broad track he had made through the snow? His mouth was bitter and harsh. Snow might cover him, but it would be no protection against bullets. If they halted and opened fire....

The Ford droned rapidly nearer, its chained tires whining on the slippery snow. He heard the motor falter and instinctively, he snatched for his automatic, lips skinning back from his teeth. But, damn it, he couldn't use his gun on police. He lay rigid, waiting. The motor picked up again, the Ford hammered on.

Wentworth crawled to the wall of the warehouse beside him, got to his feet in its shadow and ran on. The Ford was a dark blur receding down the street.

Two blocks further on, he found a taxi and flung into it. The driver turned with his hand on the meter flag, then his mouth sagged open. He, too, had recognized the Spider!

His hand snapped from the flag, darting toward his coat pocket Wentworth reached over and slapped him across the forehead with his gun. His face was like frozen steel, his eyes burning. He yanked the driver into the rear of the cab and rapidly bound and gagged him. Then he took the man's cap and operator's button and got behind the wheel.

It was clear that he could do nothing until he had got hold of a disguise, and he was without the means of creating one. There was no doubt that Nita's apartment would be watched, his also. Though he might manage to steal into the secret dressing room he had built into his penthouse, he could not risk that, now. There was not time. Already the minions of Martin might be distributing the poison.

He jammed on the gas so suddenly the taxi's tires skidded instead of taking hold. He cursed, tried again and got under way. Snow creaked beneath the rubber. A link of a chain was broken and made a regular, tinny slapping on a fender. As he pushed on uptown, with his unconscious passenger behind him, he began to run into groups of street cleaners. Thousands of unemployed had been drafted for the work. They had fires boiling up out of high cans and, clad in fagged overcoats, with their ears bound up, they leaned on snow shovels that they pushed with puffing clouds of breath. They moved slowly. Every man of them was conscious that when the snow was gone, the work and the pay ceased. They would make the snow last as long as possible.

Wentworth singled out one apart from the rest and slewed the taxi to a halt beside him.

"Want ten dollars, buddy?"

The man stopped pushing his shovel, and stared at him.

"You wouldn't kid me, mister?"

"Hop up here," Wentworth ordered and held out a bill. The man climbed in after it, standing up in the seatless space beside the driver's seat and Wentworth let him have it. The man watched him covertly, ignored the shout that came from behind.

A half-dozen blocks away, Wentworth halted the cab. "I want your clothes," Wentworth told the street cleaner. "I'll give you mine and another ten dollars to boot. Okay?"

"Lord lumme, yes!" the man gasped.

THEY MADE the exchange and the bum donned a fur-lined flying suit while Wentworth tugged into a worn-out overcoat and an ear-flap cap and wrapped a burlap sack about his throat as a muffler. It hid half his face, too.

Wentworth slopped off down the street, head down into the brash cold, until he found a subway entrance. His shoulders were slumped and his feet scuffled. Now and again he sniveled and dragged a tagged sleeve across his nose. His face was unchanged, but he doubted that police or other reward-hunters would look for him in this garb.

In the subway station, he entered a telephone booth and called Nita.

"Don't come here, Dick," she said rapidly before she even greeted him. "I'm watched. You've been indicted for Mannley's murder."

Wentworth laughed softly. "Thanks, my beautiful," he said. "I talked to Kirkpatrick. I just wanted to warn you not to take any cold medicine. It's going to be poisoned. Will you call the newspapers and tell them that? Also expose the whole thing as a racket."

He told her swiftly what had happened in Chicago.

"I don't have to call the newspapers," Nita said, acid in her voice. "I just open the door and the newspaper men fall in. But, listen, Dick dear, I think you'd better ring off now. I don't know that police aren't tapped in on my wires and they might arrest you.

"Here's some information: Your newspaper clippings show that before each poisoning outbreak, there has been a series of robberies of groceries or cosmetic shops. There haven't been any reports of drug store robberies yet."

Wentworth cried, "Good work, Nita! That's what had been worrying me. The method of distribution. Sweetheart, will you go to my apartment at once?"

Nita abruptly clicked off the telephone and Wentworth smiled wryly. That meant she had detected a listening tap and feared he might be traced. Well, he had been talking more than long enough to be traced. He glanced toward the change booth, along the empty platform. The station agent was not looking toward him. He took a single stride and leaped to the tracks, three feet below. Crouching, he ran swiftly into the darkness.

The tracks were lighted at long intervals by dim electrics. Red lights showed emergency exits and blue bulbs revealed telephones. Steel uprights marched off into the dark distances between the double line of tracks. On each side of them was the deadly third rail, carrying hundreds of volts of electricity. Distantly, he heard the humming of the rails that heralded a train. It was impossible to tell yet on which track it was.

His feet made thumping noises that echoed dimly. Abruptly, he heard voices clatter out behind him and he ducked to the right hand wall and ran on, up on his toes now for quietness. The police had done quick work in tracing that call. If the snow had not slowed their dash, he undoubtedly would have been captured already, he realized.

Peering back over his shoulder, he saw a policeman lean out with a flashlight in his hand. Wentworth flung flat down against the wall, motionless. The beam of the torch did not penetrate the darkness where he lay, but he saw the officer spring to the tracks and come toward him at a swift run. He darted a glance ahead. Another policeman coming that way. The roar of the train was heavier and he could determine that it was on the other track. He was surrounded.

WENTWORTH FELT his heart tightening within him. He was trapped by men against whom he could not fight, just when he had learned at long last how he might battle with the slaughterers.

Slowly, his face twisted in self-mockery, Wentworth drew his automatic. The police were very close now. The passage of that train howling down the tunnel would throw light upon his hiding place. For the sake of thousands of lives, the Spider was being forced to do what he had sworn he never would: Shoot down police!

He raised the pistol and his hand rubbed against cold metal that was not the track. The police had halted and were calling back and forth to each other.

Wentworth laid the automatic down and feverishly felt the metal. It was a bar three feet long, hanging on hooks against the wall. He knew what it was, a heavy, soft, iron bar with eyes in each end, which was used to hoist cars back onto the tracks when they jumped. They were placed at intervals throughout the tunnels. A germ of an idea flashed into his brain. There still was a way to escape... if it was not too late.

Quickly, Wentworth thrust the pistol back into its holster. He eased to his knees and heaved one of the bars off its hooks. His teeth clenched, his neck corded with the effort to move the heavy ingot without sound. Its weight was over a hundred pounds. He got the bar clear and lifted it vertically so that it stood upon its end before him. Then he hoisted it slowly straight upward. It was ticklish work. He dared not sway far out from the wall, lest his shadow become visible against the dim lights. The clank of the bar would betray him. Yet he must work swiftly, against the onward rush of the train.

But the need for quiet was rapidly passing. The tunnel filled slowly with the hollow roar of the speeding wheels. Wentworth got the bar high enough to get his palm under it and, balancing it on one hand, steadying it with the other, he muscled the weight upward until its lower end was shoulder high, his arm braced as for a shot-put. He staggered to his feet, let the bar begin to plunge earthward. Then, with a strong thrust of his arm, his weight behind it, he sent the bar like a javelin across the tracks toward those twin third rails. Instantly, he hurled himself flat again, panting heavily.

Wentworth literally held his breath, then there was a blinding blue-white flash of light. Electric flame leaped up in a fan from the iron bar that had flopped across the two third rails, short-circuiting a combined power of over a thousand volts. There was a hissing blast, then the bar bounded clear and darkness shut down on the tunnel. Every light save the dim blues that marked the telephones and the reds that marked the exits, widely spaced and insignificant in that Stygian gloom, blinked out. The train's brakes squealed in an emergency stop.

In the sudden silence that followed, the police shouted in frightened voices to each other. But Wentworth, alone of all those in the tunnel expecting that blinding flash, was on his feet the moment darkness shut down. In two long leaps, he sprang between the steel pillars to the opposite track and raced toward the train.

That would be the one place police would not expect him to run, toward the train whose few scattered emergency lights, battery operated, made a faint yellow spot in the darkness. He ran without sound, on his toes. The stabbing beams of the police hand-torches were scouring the spot where he had been. Within seconds, Wentworth reached the train. Crouching low, he darted past the cars to the back, there he swung up and opened the one unlocked door of the train, the one at the rear. No one noticed

117

him. The few passengers on the train had all crowded forward to stare out into the darkness, seeking the cause of the stop. Wentworth slipped in among them.

FIVE MINUTES later, the motorman had removed the bar from between the tracks, had phoned to have the current turned on again and the train clattered away. In a corner, a bum with a burlap bag for a muffler swayed and snatched a nap, his face relaxed beneath its dirt. But behind that grimy mask, Wentworth's mind was racing on to the next step in his warfare.

It still lacked two hours of dawn, the time of night when the gangsters undoubtedly would do most of their work of distributing the poison. The clippings had given him the clue. They broke into stores as burglars and took whatever of value they could find, but they did more than that. Behind them, they left the poisoned goods, whether it was canned food, acid-tainted cosmetics, or cold medicine that would stretch its users in writhing death upon the floor. If only, now, he could work with police, the gangsters might be wiped out in no time.

Somewhere in the city, during these burglaries, one criminal was sure to be spotted. If police headquarters kept on its toes and shot radio cars to the drug store where the burglary was spotted with its siren silent and orders to trail, instead of arrest the robbers… Wentworth shut his mouth grimly. Kirkpatrick would have to listen to him, that was all. He, himself, might not be able to participate, but at least he could direct the battle. As a safety precaution, Kirkpatrick could close every drug store that was burglarized pending an examination of its stock.

Leaving the train, Wentworth made a series of phone calls

from widely separated phone booths before he got the entire information in Kirkpatrick's hands.

He was reasonably sure that Kirkpatrick would follow out his suggestion, but he knew that Kirkpatrick would have to depend on the men in the radio cars to trail criminals. And that would not be easy. The prowl cars were conspicuous and there might be no opportunity for the officers to commandeer a car to do their trailing. But it was a vital work. It had to be done, if Martin's gang were to be eliminated. In Wentworth's mind, his whole plan of battle fell into neat array. The first task was to stop the medical supplies from being broadcast over the city. Police could take care of that, now that the means of distribution was apparent. The next was to locate and wipe out the men who were dealing out the poison. Police might be able to do that, but Wentworth intended to make sure by taking the field also.

He had no hope that Martin would be captured. Undoubtedly the man was still in Chicago, for there was no great need for him to rush eastward as Wentworth had. His plans were all set, his men had their orders and he could come later to reap the profits of his diabolical plot. But wiping out the gang would accomplish one thing. It would destroy Martin's one ready weapon. He would have no trouble in gathering more men to work for him, but for a while he would be forced to halt his wholesale slaughter. And before he got organized again, Wentworth thought the Spider might be able to force a settlement, if—his eyes grew hard and bleak—if police and the populace he fought to save did not before that time destroy their benefactor!

Taxis nearly all carry radios now. Some few passengers turn

them on, but chiefly they while away the waits between fares while the drivers park beside a fire hydrant with the engine running for some small warmth against the winter night's cold. Wentworth, foot-slogging through the snow, shoulders bowed, head pulled down into the muffling folds of the burlap bag, hunched up to such a cab. The driver jerked up his head from a tabloid paper and threw his arm in an angry gesture.

Wentworth opened the door and presented his automatic, muzzle first. The radio made low music at his elbow.

"Get out," Wentworth said. His voice was rough and the driver spun out like a snipe dodging a bullet. Wentworth watched him around a corner with the gun still in his hand, then got in and drove away. The cab would be reported stolen within minutes, but it was Wentworth's guess that the radio patrol cars would have something else to do this night than watch for stolen cabs. Besides, Wentworth did not expect to cover much territory. He drove a dozen blocks away and parked beside a fire hydrant, turned the radio to the wave-band of police calls. The first one that came over was a description of the taxi and himself.

"Be careful of this man," the announcer's rasping voice intoned. "He is dangerous and carries a thirty-eight caliber automatic pistol. He is believed to be Richard Wentworth, alias the Spider."

THE SHORT laugh that barked from Wentworth's lips was harsh. He had not anticipated that swift deduction. Well, Kirkpatrick had said he would prosecute the search to the last iota of his strength and ability. Wentworth settled himself deeper into the taxi seat, waiting, listening. Finally the announcement came.

"Car one-five-two, car one-fifty-two. Signal thirty at drug store, corner of Second Avenue and Harper Street. Proceed silently and follow burglars. See order two-thousand seven forty-five."

Wentworth nodded as he sped along, headed for Second Avenue and Harper Street. The order referred to would have been Kirkpatrick's general order for action when burglaries of drug stores were reported. It would direct that they follow and attempt to locate the headquarters of the poison gang. He jolted across the rutted tracks of Second Avenue and turned north. Two blocks behind him, he spotted a Ford roadster coming fast and without lights. He cursed softly to himself. If those police were on their toes, they would commandeer his cab as less conspicuous than their own car. They might identify the taxi, recall their report on "Richard Wentworth, alias the Spider."

He was still five blocks from Harper, but if the police had decided to commandeer the cab, turning into a side street would not help. The Ford came up fast, pulled alongside and a cop stuck out his head. "Pull over!" he snapped.

"Who, me?" Wentworth stammered. "What did I do?"

"You haven't done anything," said the cop. "I'm commandeering this cab."

Wentworth sighed wearily, "Okay! I hope it don't get messed up none." That sigh expressed genuine relief. If there had been a fight, it would have scared off the burglars, destroyed all his careful plans.

"Get moving," the cop ordered, "and when you get to Harper Street, go one block beyond and find a parking place."

Wentworth glanced sideways at the policeman. He was young and Irish, a broad six feet with blue eyes glinting under blond brows. He was excited and the fresh color of his face was not all from the bite of the wind. Wentworth wondered what reward Kirkpatrick had promised in that special order of his. This youngster was all keyed up.

"Want I should get the police signals?" Wentworth asked and reached through into the back compartment to work the radio.

"Good idea," grunted the cop.

He was paying no attention to Wentworth, but was staring toward where Harper Street intersected Second Avenue. He had crouched low in the empty space to keep out of sight, his visored cap laid on the floor beside him so its shield would not catch a gleam of light. He was showing rare sense, Wentworth thought. The police Ford swerved off Second Avenue, still running dark, and wallowed on east toward the river. It would cover the other end of Harper Street.

CHAPTER 13
DEATH FOR THE SPIDER!

WENTWORTH KNEW that he was sitting on a keg of dynamite. His face was not disguised and his identity was so well known, thanks to the newspapers, that a counterman in a greasy diner and a taxi driver had recognized him easily. Furthermore, the license number of this cab had been broadcast as stolen, and he was "believed" to be the thief. It was not alone for himself that he feared, though capture would be disastrous.

He thought he might be able to handle this bouncing young cop if it came to a showdown. But the chase might be endangered, and he must not miss the trail to Martin's headquarters.

If the cop identified him, he would abandon all thought of this other chase. To him, the capture of the Spider was much more important than merely trailing burglars, even if those men were tied up with a thousand murders.

So Wentworth snuggled his chin down into the protection of that scratchy muffler, watched the young policeman's bulldog profile and listened for radio reports. His cab muttered along under the elevated. He spotted a man's figure in the black shadows across from the drug store. The lookout of the burglars?

"Say, officer," he whined, "I don't know what you're looking for at Harper street, but there's a guy over on the left hand corner in the shadows."

"I see him," the cop said shortly. "Keep on past, turn the next corner and park."

"Car one-five-two. Car one-fifty-two. Call headquarters when you can. Call headquarters when you can. Do not interrupt last assignment."

The cop grunted, pulled down farther behind the steel cowling. Wentworth cranked down his window, stuck out his head and yelled, "Taxi, mister?" at the figure in the shadows.

The man did not move, but Wentworth heard the cop cursing under his breath, felt the grate of a revolver muzzle in his side. He cranked up his window and kept on, turned the next corner west.

"What's the big idea, mug?" the cop growled and his blue eyes were narrow and hard. "I believe you was tipping that guy off."

"Honest," Wentworth gulped. "Honest! If I'd sailed by without trying to get a customer, with my flag up like it is, he'd got suspicious. I was trying to help."

The cop kept the gun grinding, against his side and his eyes stayed small and hard. "You're damned smart, ain't you, mug?" he asked softly.

Suddenly, he reached out and yanked the muffler from Wentworth's face. Wentworth didn't wait to see whether he'd be identified. His hand dropped on the policeman's revolver and wedged the chamber tight with hard-gripping fingers. If that chamber didn't revolve, the hammer couldn't go back, the gun couldn't be fired. He held the chamber and lashed out with his fist.

The cop was crouching on his thighs, and in his excitement, he tried to straighten up. He caught Wentworth's blow rising and his head slammed against the roof of the cab. It batted his head down again and Wentworth snatched for his automatic. The cop hit out with his fist. Wentworth took two hard knocks in the face before he could slap the man down with the flat of his automatic.

He scanned the street behind him and saw a sedan go past fast with five men in it. With a curse, Wentworth threw open the door and rolled the cop out, thoughtfully retaining his revolver. He jerked the cab into motion with skidding tires and took the next corner so fast his rear-end slammed into banked up snow.

Wentworth was still muttering oaths as he whirled off in pursuit of the sedan. He was only guessing, of course, that it was the gangster car, but he had had another purpose in yelling at that lookout in the shadows. He had wanted to start the quarry before the other policeman or the excitement at headquarters should bungle the game.

He leaned forward and switched off his lights, swung back to Second Avenue and spotted the tail light of the sedan flickering along four blocks ahead up the middle of the street. He got outside the elevated pillars so that the long line of thick steel columns formed a screen for him and pushed on. He would be able to spot the other car if it turned off, but it was unlikely that he himself would be seen.

There was no way of telling whether that young policeman had identified him or not, but at any rate he would have police on his trail within minutes. The cop would regain consciousness quickly in the cold snow. His companion probably had seen the burglars take to their heels and would be after them. A telephoned report would set the whole network of radio cars after them.

THE CAR ahead swirled right and Wentworth braked and pivoted two blocks short of the other. When he reached the next street, he parked and waited. The sedan shot into sight and kept going east. A taxi turned south. Wentworth leaned back in his seat and pretended to be asleep. His cab was by a fire hydrant, but this was an unlikely spot for a cab stand. If his hunch was right, and the gangsters had switched to this cab… Wentworth's hands were locked upon the butts of his guns. He had the car in low gear, holding his foot on the clutch, his right on the accelerator pedal.

The taxi drifted down the street slowly, abruptly swerved out between the elevated pillars into the outer lane nearest Wentworth. He caught a glint of metal at the rear window. He had been spotted, then. He stamped the gas, yanked his foot off the clutch pedal and his cab shot forward, straight across the path of the other. Excited shots sputtered from the rear of the taxi. Wentworth heard them smack into the metal of body, heard a window crash, then he was dead across their path. He threw up his own gun and blazed away.

He blasted out his window without bothering to lower it and his first shots smacked into the rear of the other cab. He saw the chauffeur yank up a gun just as the taxi crunched into his side and he put a bullet through the man's shoulder.

But he was firing carefully. The revolver in his right hand held only two more shots. His automatic was nearly empty and that prowling police car, if it had missed the trail, could not fail to hear these shots. The still, cold air would carry the sound a mile. Wentworth flung himself toward the far side of his cab and out into the snow, circled its rear cautiously. There had been no sound, no movement from the other cab for thirty seconds. He had fired enough shots to account for every man in it, but he was by no means sure that they weren't lying in wait for him now.

But he could not hesitate. He had deliberately refrained from killing the one man in the other car that he could see clearly, the chauffeur. The chase was spoiled now, but it might not be hard to make a wounded man talk. It better not be, Wentworth told himself grimly, for the man's sake.

He went toward the other cab in a swift rush, ducking to

the protection of the taxi's own body, but no movement came from within. He yanked open the door. Still keeping under cover, he blasted one more shot into the interior and got no reply. Cautiously, he peered inside. The ceiling light had clicked on when he pulled open the door and it revealed three men in a contorted huddle on the floor and seat. Two were dead. The other had taken a bullet through his chest high up. Well, police would be here within minutes. They could take care of the wounded.

Without ceremony, Wentworth dumped the three out on the ground, shoved the semiconscious chauffeur from his seat to the floor and yanked the cab backward. It had not been damaged by the collision, taking the entire force of the blow on the bumper. Wentworth dropped from the cab then for a space of moments and daubed upon the forehead of the two dead and the one wounded gangster the seal of the Spider. There was a reckless light in his eyes. Let the police and the Underworld know that, for all the hue and cry on his trail, the Spider could still strike terribly! Let them know he still fought when any other man would have fled in terror!

He flung back into the cab and sent it roaring and skidding away. The man on the floor groaned weakly and Wentworth threw him a glance, snatched up a revolver from beside him. He whipped back to the west, past more stalling groups of snow workers, turned south on Seventh Avenue. After five blocks he cut west again and brought the cab to a halt beneath the Ninth Avenue elevated. He got out and threw a double handful of snow in the wounded man's face, rubbed it into his temples. The gangster stirred feebly, regained his senses cursing.

"Hurry up!" Wentworth said urgently. "That guy blasted the daylights out of us. Got everybody except me and you. Hurry up! Where was you going to take us?"

Wentworth was taking a chance, playing the fact that Martin had a Chicago gang. There was a chance only the chauffeur knew where to go. If it didn't work, he'd have to force the man to talk, but… He bent low over the wounded man, heard him mutter an address and grinned in triumph.

A radio in the taxi began to squawk. Wentworth straightened, listening.

"Calling all cars! Calling all cars! Richard Wentworth, alias the Spider, just killed three men at the corner of First Avenue and Thirty-second street. When last seen…" A description followed. "Bring him in, dead or alive," the order concluded.

WENTWORTH'S SHORT laugh was rasping in his throat. Killed three men, they said, and didn't explain that they were murdering gangsters who had just planted poison to kill thousands, didn't explain that the Spider had fired only in self defense, though the evidence of that must be plain upon the wrecked cab he had occupied. Well, it was not police business to justify the kills of the Spider.

Wentworth stared down at the wounded gangster on the floor of the cab. The man was conscious now, staring up wild-eyed.

"Cheez!" the wounded man gasped. "Don't hoit me, Spider, I told you what you wanted to know."

"Yeah," said Wentworth. He hauled the man into the back

of the cab and bound him tightly. Then he mounted the driver's seat and sent the taxi purring southward. The address the driver had given was on the lower east side, the headquarters of the Martin gang. At the thought his foot grew heavier on the accelerator and the cab's tires whistled and shuddered over the snow at his increased speed.

He forced himself to slow down. He could not afford to be even bawled out by a traffic policeman, not with the bullet-pocked taxi, with a wounded man in the tonneau. Wentworth realized abruptly that he was utterly worn out, recalled that he had not rested since the night before when he had slept under the professor's narcotic. He had not eaten since leaving Cleveland. The radio made a constant dinning in his ears now, orders flying thick and fast for the capture of the Spider.

Someone had spotted the fact that he had left the scene of the killing in a yellow taxi cab and radio patrolmen were ordered to halt every yellow cab and check the driver's identity. A slow anger was growing in Wentworth's heart. He was fighting for the lives of people who were trying their damnedest to kill him. He realized abruptly that he could not hope to carry his fight to a successful termination unless he ridded himself of his present garb. His ammunition, too, was nearly exhausted and there was no fresh supply in the taxi.

Slowly, unwillingly, Wentworth faced the realization that unless he wished to risk the escape of those gangsters with the consequent blow to his plans; unless he wanted to jeopardize ultimate success—which meant Martin's death—by his own capture, he must turn this phase of the battle over to police. It was madness anyway, such madness, as only the Spider could carry to a victorious conclusion, for one man to invade a head-quarters of gangsters as powerful as Martin's mob.

WENTWORTH SWERVED the yellow cab to the curb and walked hurriedly back the way he had driven, turned a corner and shambled toward a subway. His eyes quested alertly for police. A passing radio patrol car gave him an uneasy moment, but the men were occupied in stopping a yellow cab for questioning. Wentworth quickened his pace. Within minutes they would find the taxi he had abandoned and begin combing the side-streets for him. He ducked down a subway entrance and did not phone until he was well uptown.

When Kirkpatrick answered, the flat, mocking laughter of the Spider grated over the wire.

"Dick," Kirkpatrick's voice was hard, but there was a quiver in it. "Dick, for God's sake! Give yourself up, before you're killed. After that last kill of yours, after you knocked out that policeman I had to give a dead or alive order. Give yourself up, before…."

"Save your words, Kirkpatrick," Wentworth spoke still in the artificially deep voice of the Spider. "I called to give you some-thing that your bungling police almost kept me from getting, the address of the gang headquarters."

Kirkpatrick broke off his pleas. His voice came coldly over the wire as he repeated the address Wentworth gave him. "Hit them with everything you've got, Kirkpatrick," Wentworth said heavily. "I'll be seeing you."

He hung up, hurried from the booth to catch a subway train. The slump of his shoulders was not feigned now. He was tired—

tired to the soul. He had struck a blow at the gangsters who had been murdering the thousands; he had opened the way for Kirkpatrick to wipe out the lesser members of the mob. The main fight was ahead, the elimination of the steel-helmeted chief. For so long as that man remained alive, the rackets would go on. Wentworth had a plan in mind for trapping Martin, too, but it was a task to which he drove himself grimly, as to a hated duty.

It was not that he had weakened for a moment in his service of humanity. He was still as earnest as on that first day when he had pledged his life to mankind's protection against the underworld. But he knew that the end was near, even as Kirkpatrick had said. With the evidence that the Avenger had piled up against him, there could be no hope this time for the Spider. He was doomed.

Slowly, his shoulders straightened. Doomed, yes, but he would make this, his last fight, the most glorious of his life. When he went, Martin and the Avenger would go with him. The world would ring for years with the thunderous echoes of the cataclysm that had destroyed the Spider. He laughed sharply, and a pale-faced woman, lips and cheeks carrying a pallor that was not all lack of cosmetics, stared at him curiously. Wentworth arose and left the train.

Once more he shuffled through the snow, but this time he was nearing the apartment building in which he lived. There was a lightness in his feet, a rising hope in his breast, engendered by his determination that the end should find him fighting gloriously. In that secret room, he would find a haven for a few hours, until he could set the stage for the Spider's end.

Wentworth made the service entrance of the apartment building apparently without being seen. He started up service stairs and heard a man shout, heard heavy feet beat after him. He swung inside the panel of his secret room just in time and stood with his shoulders against the wall, panting heavily. His eyes were wide open, but he could see nothing in the dark.

He didn't need to see the man who had pursued to know that he was a police guard. He didn't have to be told that the guards had seen him and deliberately allowed him to enter the building to make his capture certain. Well, they would have a hard time finding this spot. Heavily, he pushed himself away from the wall and groped for a light switch, clicked it on. He crossed the room to where a black, cloth hood was attached to the wall. He put that over his head and looked through peepholes into his music room. No one was in there.

HE WENT back into the secret room. From a small refrigerator set into a wall, he took out emergency rations and ate. He stripped off his clothing then and, setting an alarm clock to ring in four hours—at noon—he flung himself down upon a bed to rest. He had done all that could be done for the present.

When he awoke, the dullness was gone from his eyes. There was a new springiness to his stride as he walked quickly about, clothing himself. When he was dressed, he dropped down before a mirror framed in a neon-light tube and went swiftly to work on his face with make-up equipment. There was once more a mocking twist to his lips. The whole city was hunting the Spider, wasn't it? Well, it would be the Spider who walked abroad this day!

Wentworth's hands moved deftly, sallowing the wind-burnt skin, building the beaked, hawk nose and painting out lips. There was a reckless fight in his eyes. They glittered with inner fires. When his disguise was complete, even to the black hat that sat low upon lank hair, the long black cape that emphasized the grotesque hunch of his shoulders, he crossed to the far wall where the cloth hood showed and put his eyes to the peepholes again.

He looked into his music room, austere, high-ceiled, its walls great gothic arches atop cathedral columns. Before a concert grand, Nita sat upon a bench. But she was not playing. Her back was to the keyboard and her smooth elbows were upon it. Her head was flung back so that the ringlets of her hair swept smoothly from her brow and she was smiling in mockery up into the face of Stanley Kirkpatrick.

There was a high lamp just behind her and it showed her face brightly even while her body was in shadow. Wentworth picked up an ear-phone connected with a microphone near the piano, and Nita's voice came to him clearly.

"I am glad to hear Dick is back in the city," she said. "Now the number of murders may decrease."

Kirkpatrick stood very erectly above her. He wore a belted overcoat and his derby and his stick were in his hand. There was a stiffness in his poise that told how weary he was.

"If Dick is in the city," he said quietly, "one sort of murder will increase: Kills by the Spider!"

Wentworth moved his head to the left and swept a glance over the rest of the room. Just inside the main doorway stood

Kirkpatrick's deputy, Marshant. His head seemed squeezed down between the breadth of shoulders that diminished his height. If this man were the Avenger, he had made a quick trip back from Chicago....

Kirkpatrick's voice came to Wentworth again. "I warned Dick that this time was the end," he said harshly, "that he would slip and be caught. And I warned him, too, that I would prosecute to the full extent of my power. I'm repeating that now to you. The evidence is air-tight. The pictures show that the man who killed Mannley wore Dick's signet on his left hand. There can be no question of a conviction."

Nita rose from her seat upon the bench. Her lounge pajamas were wine red and they emphasized her tall grace.

"What you say is ridiculous," she said swiftly. "If Dick were the Spider, he certainly would have more intelligence than to do such a thing."

Kirkpatrick looked at her without a sound. Marshant laughed harshly from his stand beside the doorway.

"He wasn't expecting the Avenger to take a picture of him," the deputy said. "And he intended to kill Mannley. It would have been quite safe."

Kirkpatrick braced his shoulders, bowed stiffly to Nita and left. Marshant lingered to laugh again, then he, too, left. Wentworth stood motionless behind the door and waited. His eyes were smiling, without mockery. Kirkpatrick had been positive that he was within hearing and he had spoken loudly so that Wentworth might hear and know the evidence that was against him. He wondered what had been the result of the attack on the gangsters. It was a difficult part that Kirkpatrick had to play, but Wentworth knew that he need expect no mercy if he fell into his friend's hands.

The smile faded and a frown took its place. The evidence was puzzling. Wentworth remembered distinctly removing the signet from his finger before he had entered Mannley's room, just as he had removed from his buttonhole the rosette of the *Légion*. Obviously, someone had done a clever piece of fake photography, but that made the evidence no less damning. The Avenger was reinforcing the evidence of the automatic.

WENTWORTH WAITED until Nita turned to the piano and began to play softly, her slender, white fingers rippling over the ivory of the keys. The silvery notes were blithe. Nita's voice came to him, a whisper into the hidden microphone near her.

"If you are there, Dick," she said, "be very careful. I am sure that the apartment is watched. There may be dictographs...."

Nita's fingers trailed off the keys. She arose and sauntered toward Wentworth's end of the room where an organ was installed. The door to the secret room Wentworth occupied was opened by patting the sound orifices of two treble tubes in a certain cadence but Nita made no move to do that. She passed close by the door, strolling.

"Thanks, my beautiful," Wentworth whispered.

He heard Nita's breath suck in sharply, but she continued strolling and passed out of sight. Wentworth pressed against the door, his arms spreading against the unfeeling wood. If only he could clasp Nita in his arms once more, then he would

go willingly to this last battle, the battle that meant the end...
Marshant stepped into the open doorway.

Behind him were two men with axes. "We heard whispering in this room," he said harshly. "There is a secret panel here somewhere and we mean to find it." He waved his arm at the ax-men. "Smash in that wall!" he pointed toward where Wentworth and Nita stood on opposite sides of the panel.

Wentworth sprang back and crossed his secret room in long strides, reached the door that opened on the stairs. Cautiously, he opened a peephole and stared out. On the platform below crouched two policemen with revolvers in their hands.

"You have no right to do this," Nita cried indignantly, and Wentworth heard her voice dimly through the panels. He ran back to peer again into his music room.

He was trapped beyond any doubt. By a strange misfortune, one of those slips that had dogged every step of his battle against Martin and the Avenger, Marshant had spotted the very panel which opened as a door. Nita's standing before it had been a clue, but it was damned clever work. He flinched back from the panel as an axe thudded dully against the other side. A muffled cry of anger rose to his lips.

Nita was still protesting, but he knew that was vain. Marshant would not be taking such drastic action unless he had a warrant. Was this then the end? Wentworth cursed himself savagely. Kirkpatrick's premonitions had got under his skin. Each time he got in a tight spot he was prepared in advance to surrender. But his anger accomplished nothing. Facts stared him in the face. The only two exits to the secret room were blocked by police with drawn revolvers, men against whom he could not fight. Yet he must escape them.

He peered once more into the music room. "This time, we've got the Spider," Marshant gloated. "The entire building is filled with my men." He drew two heavy revolvers and stood with them half-leveled at the door. The axe thudded again into the wood.

CHAPTER 14
THE SPIDER'S OATH

NITA HEARD the axes ring on steel, heard the triumphant shouts of the axe men and their redoubled blows. The burly Marshant was barking short laughter from deep in his throat. He had a revolver in each hand and he stood well back from the spot where his men hacked, stood on the balls of his feet with a readiness that Nita recognized. When that door went down, Marshant planned to go in shooting. The Spider was not going to be captured alive!

Her heart's pounding suffocated Nita. She knew that even to save his life, Wentworth would not shoot at police. He might slug or fire over their heads, but his swift deadly bullets were not for the defenders of the law. What could she do? Was she to stand here helplessly while Dick was murdered? For murder it would be as surely as if he did not have a weapon in his secret room.

Nita smiled and stood away from the wall against which she

had been leaning, strolled across the room as casually as the Spider could have managed.

"I suppose you're prepared to pay damages on all this, Mr. Marshant," she said, taking a cigarette from a case on the piano, lighting it.

Marshant barked his sharp laughter. "I'll pay it out of the reward money," he snorted.

Nita's laughter tinkled. "That, I believe, is what is known as counting the hens a bit before the incubation." She strolled to a high arched stone fireplace and tapped ashes into the hearth, stood staring down at the unlighted logs. She dropped a hand carelessly beside her and it closed about the handle of a heavy poker. A glance from the corners of her eyes showed that a single leap would put her within striking distance of Marshant. Then she waited, watching the work of the axe men. They had stripped aside all the wood now and were prying tentatively at the edges of the steel door.

One of them gave a violent wrench and the steel plate snapped aside into the facing. A choked shout rasped in Marshant's throat and he lunged forward, guns swinging up. Nita made her leap, the poker sweeping in an arc. Then both man and woman checked in midspring and Nita screamed. She darted forward, but Marshant's hand closed on her shoulder, thrust her roughly aside.

"No, you don't," he said harshly. "None of your tricks."

Nita pitched to her hands and knees and stayed that way, her head wrenched up, her eyes staring. The two policemen shrank back from the opening into which light streamed from the music room. Something dark and horrible swung limply in the doorway, something that turned slowly to left and to right, but had no other movement.

"It's a dummy," Marshant swore.

"No, chief," gulped a policeman. "It's *him!* He's committed suicide!"

They went slowly toward the figure of the Spider, hanged by the neck in the doorway. A chair had been knocked over and lay beneath his feet. His eyes bulged and his face was purple with congested blood, tongue pinched between his teeth. Marshant cursed suddenly and leaped forward to fling his arms about the Spider and lift him down. If he were not yet dead, Marshant wanted the glory of capturing him alive. The policemen crowded in behind him.

Abruptly, movement convulsed the Spider. Both his feet lashed out and caught Marshant in the stomach. The burly deputy doubled forward and sat down heavily and Wentworth dropped lightly to his feet, a blade slashing above his head to cut the rope. The policemen cursed, surging backward and squeezing together in the open doorway. They sought frantically to flee from the dead man who attacked them, the dead man whose face was still purplish with strangulation, whose tongue still pinched out between his teeth. Wentworth's able fists took care of them both. He stepped back and thoughtfully slapped Marshant across the base of the skull with a blackjack, then he snatched off the fearful mask made from implements of disguise, that had covered his features.

Nita surged to her feet and plunged toward him, flung her

139

"It's a dummy!" Marshant swore.

"No, Chief," a policeman gulped,

"it's him—it's the Spider!"

arms about his neck. "Ah, Dick, Dick!" she sobbed. "That was cruel!"

AN END of the rope still dangled from inside the collar of his cape. It was fastened beneath his arm pits. Wentworth laughed lightly.

"Cruel, but rather necessary," he told her, holding her tightly. "If it hadn't been for your scream, they might have shot first and investigated afterward. Now, I've got to go, darling."

"The building is full of police," Nita said rapidly. "Every exit and every floor is guarded. How can you go?"

Wentworth shrugged. "I've got to."

He ripped off his cape and hat, picked up an overcoat that one of the policemen had discarded to work, jerked on the uniform cap.

"Go into the secret room," he said, "and when policemen leave the stairs, open the door and step out."

"But you!"

"I'll join you there."

While Nita stepped over the prone bodies of the police, Wentworth ripped out the telephone to prevent an alarm, then he raced to the outer door with pounding feet.

"Quick!" he yelled into the hall. "I've got the Spider, but he's fighting!"

He left the door open and ducked into the cover of the portières. He shouted hoarsely, grunted as if he struggled. He heard cries in the hall and the rapid pound of feet. Police raced toward the arched door of the music room. Wentworth slipped out into the hall and shut the door, wedged it fast with a bit of rasp steel. Nita walked toward him rapidly along the hall, drawing a cloak about her shoulders.

"I jammed the secret door shut," she said.

Wentworth nodded and signaled his private elevator. It rose swiftly while police pounded on the door of his apartment. A cop was running the cage and he gawped at the muzzle of an automatic staring him in the eyes.

"Down," Wentworth ordered casually.

The cage descended and as it stopped at the bottom floor, Wentworth sapped the policeman operator and opened the door himself. Nita sauntered out first into a ring of four police. There were two more at the outer door, another pair at the foot of the steps. She looked at them disdainfully, jerked her arm away when Wentworth touched it.

The deception worked for two seconds, until Wentworth was within reach of the four police. Even as they gasped with realization of the trick, Wentworth was in motion. Blackjacks slipped from each sleeve into the palm of his hands and, both arms striking, he charged the four.

"Save me! Save me!" Nita cried. She ran toward the two stair guards with her arms stretched out beseechingly. They bounded to meet her and she gripped an arm of each desperately. Needled rings she had picked from Wentworth's supplies in the secret room did their work and the two men stood foggily, then reeled back against the wall, already somnolent with narcotics.

One cursed, "You dirty little tramp!" He tried to raise his gun and Nita took it from his fumbling fingers.

Three of the police Wentworth had attacked were down now,

143

but the other two from the doorway were closing in warily. They carried guns in their hands, but they hesitated to use them. After all, this man in a police uniform had fired no shots.

Nita leveled her captured gun. "Hands up!" she ordered sharply.

The cops cursed, their heads jerking toward her. Wentworth heaved up and dived at their legs. One man came down with both of his knees in Wentworth's side. The other reached out and slapped with the muzzle of his gun. It dug into Wentworth's shoulder. He gasped with pain, wrenched and tumbled the two men together. Nita sprang in and struck with the reversed revolver and one cop collapsed.

Wentworth reeled to his knees, then to his feet, slugging powerfully. The other policeman went down. He was still in the air, falling, when a blinding flash of light filled the hallway. **FOR AND** instant, it froze Wentworth and Nita in rigid surprise; then he was plunging toward two men in civilian clothes who stood by the outer doors, a reporter he recognized and a newspaper photographer whose flashlight had startled them. The photographer was already in motion, fleeing with his camera. The reporter remained to fight, but went down at the first blow.

Nita at his heels, Wentworth plunged through the outer doors to the street and saw a taxi spurt from the curb, snow flying from its wheels. He spun, hunting another, and saw two more police pounding toward him from a parked radio roadster with guns glinting in their hands.

"The chief wants that guy!" Wentworth shouted, pointing after the fleeing taxi. "He snapped a picture, and…."

The cops raced up to him, staring at the fugitive taxi and Wentworth's two blackjacks flicked out. He sprang over their falling bodies to the police roadster and sent it racing and skidding up the street. Nita huddled beside him, shoulders hunched from the biting cold. She crowded as close to Wentworth as his wild driving would permit. There was a small, happy smile on her lips.

"Now, Dick," she said. "You can't disappear without me. We're outlaws together."

Wentworth skated around a corner in a shower of snow, heard the rising wail of sirens behind. His face was set in a hard, grim mold. Unless he could recover that photograph, what Nita prophesied was absolute truth. She was bound in outlawry with him, assisting a murderer to escape police.

He spun another corner, speeding toward the offices of the *Globe,* for it had been a reporter of that newspaper who had helped the camera man to escape. Two things to do at once, escape the police and recover that photograph. He wove around two more corners and slammed on brakes. The Ford spun completely about, bumped a snow bank and halted. A taxi was stalled in the middle of the street. By the side of it, the camera man whom Wentworth pursued stood cursing and shaking his fist down the street.

Wentworth spilled from the police car with an automatic in his hand.

"Where's that photograph?" he demanded.

"The Avenger!" snarled the newspaper man. "The Avenger held me up and took it!"

Wentworth heard what the reporter said with a sense of disbelief. The Avenger? But he was in Chicago, or had been twenty-four hours ago, blocked off from the East by the break-down of all communications in the blizzard. But there was no time to speculate on that. Police were on his heels. He hurled back to his car and it leaped away with whining tires as he sprang to the running board. Nita had taken the wheel.

Wentworth hurled a swift question at her. "Three planes got through from the west," she told him, "and they're hoping to get trains through by night. The need for foodstuffs, you know. They performed miracles in clearing the way."

Then the Avenger might have come on any of those planes. He recalled abruptly that the weather had been clearing when he had left Buffalo. It had been only necessary to arrange for a take-off and a landing and the planes could come through. But his battle eastward had not been in vain. Because he had reached New York early, Kirkpatrick had been prepared to stop the sale of medicines and he himself had learned the location of the gang headquarters.

His mind flicked back to the photographer. Needless to speculate on the Avenger's purposes. He had simply added another item to his evidence against the Spider. And this time, he had involved Nita also. And the Avenger had known uncannily where to strike. He seemed almost to have arranged for the picture to be taken… Wentworth recalled sharply that the taxi beside which the photographer had stood had had no driver.

That was the explanation then. The Avenger had posed as a taxi driver.

"Find an alley, dear, and park," Wentworth said swiftly. "We've got to get rid of this car."

While the car twisted and skated on icy streets, Wentworth made slight changes in his face. It had been well enough to defy the city in the garb of the Spider alone, but with Nita beside him, the situation changed. He made himself as inconspicuous as possible. Nita found an alley and charged the police car over a two-foot barrier of snow before it stalled. Wentworth led her rapidly to a subway station and they sped northward.

He had not lied when he had stated that everything was prepared for his disappearance. He had an apartment in the west eighties rented under an assumed name and it was to this he took Nita. In the small, plainly furnished living room, he relieved her of the long coat that had concealed her lounging pajamas, then faced her, his lips gravely smiling. Nita faced him joyously. Her violet eyes were sparkling.

"Now, Dick," she said, "you will have to take me with you when you disappear. You can't leave me behind to face the charges alone. If the Avenger has that plate...."

HER VOICE died as Wentworth continued to gaze down at her with compassion in his eyes. He lifted a hand and stroked the clustering chestnut curls, lifted her chin and pressed a light kiss upon her lips.

"Dick, what is it?" Nita asked him swiftly. "You have everything ready to disappear, haven't you? Nothing has happened to destroy your funds?"

Wentworth's mouth twisted. He opened his eyes and blinked away the blur that was before them and turned to face Nita again, cupping her dear face in his hands, fighting down the pain that was like a twisted knife in his heart.

"I hate to tell you, my darling," he said gently. "But... it just can't be."

"Why?" she asked.

Wentworth took his hands away from her face and whirled to pace up and down the room.

"The evidence against me is complete," he said. "The Avenger has enough a dozen times over to send me to the chair. Every man and woman I pass on the street recognizes me and says, 'There goes the Spider!' All Kirkpatrick's police are hunting me with orders to bring me in 'dead or alive.'"

"I know all that, Dick," Nita's voice was deadly still, stripped of all emotion. "I know all that but none of it would keep you from disappearing. Your plans are well laid."

"Do you suppose I haven't told myself that ten thousand times?" he asked sharply, his voice close to cracking. "But the leader of this damnable conspiracy is still alive. And I don't know him. There is only one way to find him out."

"Still alive!" It was a cry from Nita. "But the police smashed them this morning. Kirkpatrick was fair about it. He told the newspapers that you had given him the address. They killed twelve men, captured five or six more with packets of poisoned cold medicine on them."

Wentworth nodded. It was good to hear, but it was not enough.

Martin, damn him, was still alive, and while he lived, there could be no safety for the nation's millions. He need only whisper his dread threats and industry would bow to him. And now and again, when his hold threatened to slip, he would kill another thousand persons, or destroy another thousand women's faces. Nita was walking toward him, her deep, tragic eyes gazing into his.

"What are you trying to tell me, dear?" she asked quietly.

Wentworth still stood rigidly, hands clenched. "Just this," he said between clenched teeth. "That while that fiend is alive, I cannot disappear. I cannot run to safety. And to capture him means... the end!"

"But why, dear, why?" Nita's calmness broke. She was clinging to him suddenly, imploring him with piteous eyes. "Happiness seems so near, sweetheart. We have always realized that some day, the chase would grow too hot, that you would have to go away. Sometimes, when I was weak and lonesome, I have prayed that the day might come. And now it has come."

"And I cannot go!" Wentworth's voice was harsh. "Would you have the Spider turn his back on a living enemy?"

Nita took her hands from his coat. She looked down at them and twined her white slim fingers together. She drew a deep breath and it made a shuddering noise in her throat.

"Yes, Dick," she whispered. She looked up at him and now her fists were clenched at her sides, her chin was up. "Yes, Dick," she said clearly. "I would have you run away. You have done enough for humanity. You have risked your life and given of your strength and brain without stint for years. You have saved

149

thousands of lives, millions. You have saved your country time and again. And how humanity has repaid you?"

There was bitterness and anger in Nita's bearing. "How has humanity repaid you?" she repeated, her voice was like a challenging trumpet. "I'll tell you how: By hounding you until you are in deadly peril even when you walk along the street; by forcing police to spend their time hunting for you with drawn guns, instead of running down criminals; by putting a sixty-thousand-dollar price on your head!"

WENTWORTH LIFTED a hand wearily. "Does that matter?" he asked gently. "I do not serve humanity for a reward. I serve that men may have happiness, that the vultures of crime may be purged from the earth. The service is reward in itself."

He shook his head as Nita would have gone on. "Darling," he said, "Martin must die before we can go. And the only way to trap him is to offer myself once more as bait, and to do it publicly. If I can do that and still escape, I shall do it… but I can see no hope at all."

The anger was gone from Nita now, but she still stood rigidly. Slow, big tears were sliding down her cheeks.

Hoarsely, Wentworth cried: "For God's sake, Nita, don't—" He stood on braced feet, hands clenched. "Don't!" he repeated tightly. "God, Nita, I'm human as well as you. Don't you suppose that sometimes this gets to be almost more than I can bear? Don't you know that sometimes the torture of the service I have sworn tears at my heart?"

"Your heart, yes," Nita said bitterly, "but never your mind. Oh, Dick, don't you see? It's the sheer ingratitude of it all. Humanity hating you. And you giving your life, and more than your life. Your heart rebels, yes, but always the mind—the mind of the Spider, Dick, not that of Richard Wentworth—will not yield."

Wentworth's shoulders sagged. He stared down at the floor, lifted a hand to his weary head, pressing, pressing against the ache there. No, he would never yield! His heart ached, too. Suddenly Nita was in his arms, her lips lifted for his kiss.

"Forgive me, Dick," she said quietly. "I won't do it again. It's just that sometimes...."

Wentworth took her close to his heart, buried his face in her fragrant hair.

A thunderous crash, a smashing tinkle of broken glass jerked up his head, but he made no move to seize his weapons. It was useless. Two policemen with leveled guns crouched in the window they had broken. The door hung crazily by one hinge and in the opening stood Kirkpatrick. He strode into the room and from behind him darted Patsy Malone, her eyes glittering with hate.

"You are under arrest, Dick," Kirkpatrick's voice was utterly without expression, "for the murder of Mannley."

Patsy Malone flung back her head and laughed. The laughter changed into a sob.

"And may you burn in hell for ten thousand years!" she shrilled. "You killed my Shane!"

CHAPTER 15
JACKSON INTERFERES

WENTWORTH PUT Nita aside slowly, still staring at the mixture of grief and triumph on the Irish girl's face. His mind still besotted with his own struggle. He was exhausted emotionally. He could only think dully that the end had come sooner than he had thought. Now his plans for Martin could not be fulfilled, that man would continue to prey upon the people. He jerked his head angrily. This was nonsense. Had someone cast a spell over him that he conceded defeat so easily?

Granted that he was captured, that there was no way to escape, did that mean the end? He flung his mind at the problem. "Oh, Kirk," Nita was saying. "Couldn't you have allowed us this one last little moment?"

Kirkpatrick was bowing gravely, with his perpetual studied grace. Courteous regret was on his face, and his eyes were haggard. "I am sorry, Nita," he said.

That was all. Wentworth knew that Kirkpatrick had done much for him in making the capture himself. If it had been any one else the capture would have been made in the smoke of blasting guns that would have torn the life out of his body. But he must think of other things than this.

Patsy Malone said that her brother was dead and she blamed him for it. Well, he might not be dead. But that was unimportant, it was obvious that she had led police to this hideout. She could have got information as to his whereabouts only from Jackson. That was clear, too. He shook his head sadly. Jackson had failed him utterly. The man was either a traitor or a feeble dupe in this girl's hands.

He looked to Kirkpatrick and found the Commissioner's eyes alertly upon him.

"Kirk," he said desperately, "I must talk with you in private. I give you my parole not to attempt to escape during that time."

Kirkpatrick looked at him with cold, dead eyes and shook his head. "You are a prisoner, Dick," he said flatly, "and you must take a prisoner's treatment."

"The Commissioner would listen to important information from any prisoner." Wentworth argued anxiously. "As to my parole, you do not need to accept that. Police can keep guard just out of hearing."

Kirkpatrick hesitated, then shrugged agreement. "It will do no good, but you may talk."

He walked with Wentworth to a corner of the room. "Now what is it?"

Wentworth drew a deep breath, his eyes holding his friend's. "I have a plan to catch both the Avenger and Martin, the gangster behind these poisonings."

Kirkpatrick waited, saying nothing, his eyes fixed on Wentworth's face.

"My plan is this," Wentworth continued rapidly. "The Avenger has agreed to meet me at any time and place I name. I want to arrange that and let Martin know the plans. He is anxious to remove us both, and will, I am sure, come after us. The rest should be easy."

"You want me to release you for this—meeting?" Kirkpatrick's voice was heavy.

WENTWORTH SHOOK his head, smiling wanly. "No, nothing as impossible as that, Kirk. I only ask that you make the arrangements as I wish, and that at the proper time you allow me to go to the spot under surveillance—under guard of any number of men you can hide. And that, once on the scene, you allow me a free hand. I promise you that when the affair is ended, I will surrender to you."

Kirkpatrick was silent for a long time. Wentworth pleaded with him, pointing out how Martin could reorganize, and the total lack of clues to his identity. Ultimately Kirkpatrick agreed. "I want your pledge not to attempt to escape, Dick," he replied.

"You have it," Wentworth said simply.

Kirkpatrick's eyes met his sternly. "I'm risking everything, Dick," he said slowly. "I could never justify this, even to myself if there were a slip-up."

A faint smile touched Wentworth's lips. His face was very pale. "You're not risking anything, Kirk," he said slowly. "If my plans fail, you'll still have a prisoner and your evidence."

Nita was giving a fine exhibition of mass disdain. Apparently she saw neither the policeman, nor the gloating Patsy Malone. Only when Wentworth walked toward her, she smiled.

"Tonight, dear," he said, "you will receive a message from me. Follow it implicitly."

Her eyes questioned but got no answer. She looked to Kirkpatrick. "You mean you aren't taking me along, too?" she asked.

"There are no charges against you, Nita," Kirkpatrick said

kindly. Then they filed out, taking Wentworth with them. Nita watched them go and for long after they had left, her eyes remained fixed on the door that sagged from one twisted hinge. Finally, she gathered her courage and went home to her apartment on Riverside Drive. Men and women turned curiously as she alighted from the taxi and walked across the walk. Even for these days when women dared use no cosmetics, she was strangely pale. Even the reporters clustered about her door gave way without a question.

Ram Singh awaited her. He had discovered the police at his master's apartment and reported to her instead. He had found that all the suspects Wentworth had named, save only one, had been in New York throughout the time the Avenger had been operating in Chicago. The exception was Commander Samuels. He had dropped from sight for days together.

Scarcely was the report finished when the telephone rang insistently. Jackson calling from Chicago. He had made the trip west to help Wentworth. Communications had just been restored.

"I sent this information to New York by Patsy Malone by plane last night," Jackson said. "Hers was the first plane to go through after the storm. I tangled with Martin's men and got wounded, but I learned they are planning to use the poison in candy bars next."

"Did you give Patsy Malone Mr. Wentworth's secret address?" Nita asked, surprised at her calmness of voice.

"I had to," Jackson said swiftly. "I was afraid she wouldn't find him at home."

"Patsy Malone took the police there," said Nita in clear sylla-bles. "Mr. Wentworth is now under arrest, charged with murder."

The wire hummed silently between them after that... The operator broke to find if they were through talking and Jackson said hurriedly. "No, no!" There was another pause.

"Patsy took the police there?" he asked heavily. "You are sure?"

"I was there when they arrived," Nita said.

Jackson's voice dropped a full tone. "Will you give the warning about candy to the police? I'm flying to New York. Good-bye."

NITA DID not know how much later it was that Ram Singh brought her newspapers with great screaming headlines across the front page:

WENTWORTH ARRESTED AS SPIDER!

The story narrated that the Avenger had phoned the infor-mation but that Commissioner Kirkpatrick refused to comment on the report. The Avenger had also said that it had been he who had directed police to Wentworth's hiding place; that he had turned over to police irrefutable evidence. A knot like a fist caught in Nita's throat and her breath got past it with difficulty.

NITA VAN SLOAN

Did that mean the automatic that had killed Mannley? She read on, but the paper gave no details.

This great spread of news had crowded into a single column a new outbreak of the poison deaths, this time traceable to cold medicine. Despite embargoes and newspaper warnings, the toll for New York City was over a thousand. She skimmed on through that story. Throughout the United States, these mysterious poisonings were spreading. Seven thousand had died this day. The causes were various: canned meats, and fish; medicine; package food of all varieties.

Nita read these facts without emotion. She became conscious of the fact that Ram Singh stood unobtrusively against the wall with arms folded, his hawkish eyes impassive beneath his turban-wrapped brow. He, too, was waiting. Nita sprang to her feet and began to pace the floor.

When the phone bell pealed finally, Nita stood and stared at the instrument for moments before she picked it up. The smooth, hard rubber felt cool and she realized her hands were fevered.

"Dick, darling," she said.

"Don't sound so mournful, sweetheart," Wentworth's voice was hearty. "Here's what you must do. Insert an ad in the Times personals for the morning, addressed to Mannley. It should read this way: Tonight at midnight in the Waldorf-Astoria, Main ballroom, unless you are the coward your actions indicate. No signature. Got it?"

Nita repeated the message breathlessly. "What does it mean, Dick?"

Wentworth laughed sharply. "It's a challenge to the Avenger. Send Ram Singh to give the same word to Patsy Malone."

"But, Dick," Nita hesitated. "How will you be able to meet the Avenger? How did you get to a phone?"

"I'm in Kirk's office," Wentworth's voice went emotionless. "We have an agreement. I'll see you at the Waldorf. Don't forget to get word to Patsy Malone. Ram Singh can carry the message. 'Bye, darling."

Nita groped twice for the phone cradle before she found it. Her eyes refused to focus on the instrument. Her heart was beating strongly, like a noisy drum in her throat. Was it possible that even in the face of doom, her Dick had found a way? But she dared not let herself hope. The Avenger's evidence was too much. And Wentworth had given his parole not to escape. He would not break his word. No, there was no hope. But her heart continued to sing and Nita felt a strange jubilance as she set about doing the things that Wentworth had requested. She even managed to sleep....

SOON AFTER dawn, Jackson's ringing of the bell awoke her. She wrapped a long black robe about her and went into the living room to see him. She felt hatred of him tightening her heart. This was the man whose bungling had helped to doom her Dick.

Jackson's wide-jawed square face was pale, but he seemed solid on his feet, and his eyes were like live coals.

"Where is the Major?" he asked. His voice was quiet enough but it sounded forced out of his throat.

"In jail," Nita told him shortly. "Tonight at midnight he duels the Avenger. He wants to make sure that Martin hears of that fact. He desired that Patsy Malone hear of it, too." She masked her hatred, but her bitterness crept out. "Do you think you could get word to her?" she asked almost sweetly.

Jackson made no reply to her last phrase. "How is he to get out of jail for the duel?"

Nita shook her head. "He has made some sort of deal with

Kirkpatrick. There is no doubt that the duel means his death. You read the newspapers?"

Jackson nodded his head woodenly. His face continued impassive. "Thank you, Miss Nita," he said, about-faced and stalked for the door.

"What are you going to do, Jackson?" Nita asked sharply.

"I'm going to see the Major," he told her from the door.

Wentworth was in conference with Kirkpatrick when Jackson was announced. Kirkpatrick nodded jerkily, "In a moment," he said. "Are all our plans complete now, Dick?"

Wentworth checked over a list before him. "Every one of the suspects has been notified to attend," he said slowly. "Patsy Malone will be there all right, hoping to see her brother avenged. I'm depending on Martin learning of this through her; or through the ad. There can't be much doubt that he is in town. Certainly the capture of his men will set him to organizing a fresh gang."

"It sounds as complete as possible, Dick," Kirkpatrick said gravely, "but I am very dubious of success." He pressed a button and a policeman thrust in a carrot-topped head. "Let Jackson come in!"

Kirkpatrick had aged years in recent days. The deep-cut lines about his mouth corners were chiseled permanently into his face. Even his mustaches, usually sharply pointed, seemed to droop with age. He looked up heavily, both hands flat on the desk, as Jackson came in. The door closed and Jackson leveled a heavy gun.

"Please do not move, Mr. Kirkpatrick, sir," he said. He was polite, but there was menace in his voice.

"Put that gun up, Jackson," Wentworth snapped.

"Sorry, Major," said Jackson, his face impassive. "You're getting out of here."

"Put that gun up," Wentworth repeated. "I've given my parole."

"I haven't," Jackson replied.

Wentworth sprang toward him, snatching for the gun and Jackson dodged and slapped and Wentworth collapsed unconscious. Kirkpatrick had started to his feet, his hand going to a gun in his drawer. Before he could level it, Jackson knocked him out, too. Jackson was breathing deeply through his nose. It made small hissing noises. He crossed to the door and listened there, then he shifted his gun to his left hand and got Wentworth up on his right shoulder and stalked out of the door.

The carrot-topped cop gasped and went down with a gun-welt across his forehead. Jackson descended to the basement in the elevator with his gun in the operator's side, slugged the man there and carried Wentworth out of the door where patrol wagons delivered their charges.

He went passed a room where men were vehemently intent over pinochle. They didn't look up, didn't heed the starting purr of an automobile motor. Kirkpatrick's phone call was minutes late.

NURSING HIS aching head in his hands, Kirkpatrick sat behind his desk and stared down at the blotter. He had had one flash of doubt concerning Wentworth, then that had died. If

Dick had given his pledged word, then he had not connived this subterfuge to evade that pledge and he had attempted to seize Jackson. No, Jackson had acted on his own.

Abruptly, Kirkpatrick jerked up his head. Jackson was infatuated with Patsy Malone. It had been Jackson, indirectly, who had betrayed Wentworth's hiding place. Was it possible that in kidnapping his Master, he had been working for the Avenger?

A sharp fear stabbed through Kirkpatrick. He had fought to put Wentworth behind the bars, but through every minute of the fight he had hoped that his friend would in some way elude him. It had been with a sinking heart that he had accepted the surrender in that hideout Patsy Malone had revealed, and there had been hatred in his heart for the Irish girl.

He was conniving a violation of the law in permitting Dick to meet the Avenger tonight and he had done it willingly. Not so much to trap Martin and the Avenger, but in the hope that Dick might find a clean death and not be forced to go through the humiliation of trial and prison and execution. If Wentworth could achieve that, Kirkpatrick felt that he would be willing to accept whatever punishment was meted out to him for his part in the affair.

Kirkpatrick flung himself from his desk and paced his office floor with long, angry strides. He hurled the full forces of the police force into a search for Wentworth. At eleven o'clock, one hour before the scheduled meeting, he had learned precisely nothing. He left his home with an aching heaviness in his breast to take Nita to the Waldorf-Astoria, to the scene of the duel Wentworth had planned and now, perhaps, might never fight....

CHAPTER 16
THE AVENGER'S TRICK

THROUGHOUT THE long day, Nita had gone emptily about her apartment, doing unimportant things as if they were the most important things in the world. She had spent a half hour feeding Apollo who was more than capable of feeding himself. She ironed lace which her maid could have prepared more prettily. For an hour she sat before her easel trying to mix the exact shade of a sunset cloud. Ram Singh watched her from his motionless post against the wall, and his eyes were brooding.

Nita had dragged through days before this when Wentworth's life hung in the balance, but never before, even when her Dick had been reported dead, had she known such an utter sense of futility and despair. Dick himself had given up. He was carrying on the battle to its bitter end, but not with any hope of escaping from the doom that overshadowed him. He hoped merely to do humanity one last service before he died.

And now Jackson had interfered even with that plan, as he had bungled so many others. Nita turned her eyes toward the ice-spotted river, but she did not see it. There was a prayer in her heart, a prayer she had never thought it necessary to say before for the all-powerful Spider: *Dear God, help Dick!*

When Kirkpatrick came, she went with him woodenly, her head held high and pridefully. A newspaper man whispered audibly to a companion.

"Marie Antoinette goes to her tumbrel," he snickered.

163

The other newspaper man shoved him violently against the wall and went toward him with his fists clenched.

"Keep your mouth shut," he snarled.

Nita heard all that in a vague way, but she ignored them as Kirkpatrick did. Loud-mouthed wrangling rose behind them as the elevator descended.

"Do they know anything?" Nita asked.

Kirkpatrick shook his head. He was frowning at the closed door.

"No one knows anything," he said slowly. "I called a conference to discuss means of combating the poisoners and promised to present such witnesses as might prove useful. It's a committee of citizens who are demanding action by the city, an end of the poison deaths. Dick decided to use them. In underworld circles, we had it whispered that both the Spider and the Avenger would be there. By that means, Dick hopes to lure this man, Martin, into a trap. He says that Martin is anxious to dispose of the Avenger."

They were in Kirkpatrick's car now, purring eastward between head-high banks of dirty snow. It was five minutes of twelve when they entered the Waldorf and took an elevator directly to the ball room. Nita paced through the familiar halls with a sense of utter unreality. It seemed a flimsy trap that her Dick had built and now he might not even be there to lend it the strength of his own keen mind.

She was abruptly sure that there was much more to the plan than Kirkpatrick had said, perhaps more than he knew. Wentworth did not usually confide his full plans to anyone. Strangely, that gave her hope. It gave her the courage to walk, quietly smiling, past a group of newspaper men near the ballroom door. She even inclined her head to Eddie Blanton, puffing nervous bursts of smoke from his long cigarette holder. He seized the opportunity to stride forward.

"I say, Kirkpatrick," he said in a whisper. "What's going on here tonight? There's more afoot than just giving evidence to this bunch of mugs that call themselves the Committee of Public Safety. Anyway, you've been refusing to see any of them, and now, all at once, you promise to put all your cards on the table."

"A matter of public policy, or politics," Kirkpatrick told him with a slight smile.

"Will you bring Wentworth here tonight to testify?" Blanton asked. "The Avenger phoned us he would be here, but that he didn't want it published before-hand."

Nita studied the reporter's shrewd, horsey face, so incongruously set on heavy shoulders, and felt a sudden distaste for the man. It was not his cocky self-assurance. That was an air that went with his job, a necessary adjunct to crashing in where he wasn't wanted. It was his sly satisfaction when he mentioned Wentworth. She recalled that Dick had said Blanton had long suspected him.

Kirkpatrick jerked a hand impatiently. "Would you mind stepping aside, Blanton?" He gestured Nita toward the broad, double doors.

"We know you've got Wentworth a prisoner, Kirkpatrick," Blanton clung to the commissioner's elbow. "Why not admit it?"

KIRKPATRICK LIFTED his chin in a gesture toward a

The Spider whirled toward the Avenger. "Come, Ivan,"

his voice rang clearly, "draw your saber!"

quiet man in tuxedo who stood just inside the doors. The man strode alertly forward, and Blanton fell back with a laugh. Nita and Kirkpatrick went in and were immediately the center of attention. Heads turned on all sides and a boy in a light-blue uniform hurried forward, clicked his heels and reported that Commander Samuels wished to speak to him on the platform.

Nita's hand had been resting on Kirkpatrick's arm. Her fingers closed tightly upon it.

"But Kirk," she was a little breathless. "Is he on the committee?" She knew Wentworth suspected Samuels of being the Avenger.

Kirkpatrick nodded, his eyes veiled as they met hers. "Commander Samuels was in naval intelligence," he told her without expression. "He has been called in as a consultant by the committee."

Nita felt once more a sense of great things that were impending—things that would be unexpected and terrible. Her breasts were stirring with sharply accented breathing and she looked about her, half tearfully, seeking the reason. Blanton had felt it, too. She found that once more she was gripping Kirkpatrick's arm painfully. Her fingers ached with the tension.

Kirkpatrick seated her and hurried off with a deliberate bow. His face was expressionless as he strode toward the platform. Nita followed him with her eyes, saw the men assembled there. Commander Samuels was rising, ruddy faced wreathed in smiles as usual, the blond hyphens of his eyebrows raised. Something was utterly incongruous about his formally clad figure, but for the moment Nita could not place it. She saw then that, after the manner of service men, he wore high shoes instead of the proper oxfords or pumps.

Deputy Commissioner Marshant stood upon the platform talking with Kirkpatrick and Commander Samuels. The broad bulk of the two would have dwarfed a less commanding man than Kirkpatrick, but there was an arrogance in his carriage that dominated despite his lesser stature. Nita's eyes left them and turned to the audience.

Patsy Malone was directly opposite her in another bank of seats. Although she had known the Irish girl would be here, she felt anger sending a flush up her cheeks. That was the woman who, through Jackson, had trapped Wentworth.

On Patsy's right sat a man who almost cringed in his seat. It was absurd, but he held a baby in his lap. Nita recalled Wentworth's story of his fight with the Avenger in Patsy's apartment. That man would be the neighbor, Coxwell. A few seats away was a man with a stony, pasty-white face. He seemed to see everything yet look at nothing. Nita placed him, too: the croupier, Larue, from Mannley's gambling halls.

At a long table to one side near the front, newspaper men lounged in their chairs and smoked. Eddie Blanton, with studied insolence, had hooked his heels over a corner of the table. He snapped them down when he caught her eyes and sauntered forward, his horsey face longer than usual, smoke streaming over his shoulder from his foot-long cigarette holder. Curiously, Nita noticed that he was knock-kneed.

Blanton leaned over her confidentially. "What's coming off

here tonight?" he whispered. "Something big's in the wind. My nose for news tells me that."

Nita continued to smile. She crossed her knees and tapped a cigarette on the knee cap. "Have you a match, Mr. Blanton?" BLANTON LIT her cigarette with an exaggerated bow and walked purposefully toward the platform. The newspaper man was restless as a hound before the hunt.

A woman screamed.

Nita jerked her head to the right, staring at a woman who had half-risen in her seat. She was pointing and she had clapped a hand to her mouth, partly smothering her cry. Men had started to their feet. Their heads jerked, too, to the spot where she pointed, the platform.

A quiver shook Nita as her eyes took in the scene. Against the proscenium arch at one side of the stage leaned a man with a sub-machine gun in his arms. He had a black mask over his eyes and the gun's muzzle moved slowly back and forth over the assemblage.

"Don't move," the man said clearly, "and you won't be hurt."

Nita's eyes flicked from him to the other men on the stage. In a confused group, they were being herded off the platform, down a short flight of stairs and out into the audience. Behind them were three more masked men and as the last of the group descended, she saw that they, too, carried machine guns. Kirkpatrick still stood on the bottom step. "Don't attempt to shoot it out with them," he said in a quiet voice that carried to the far corners of the room. "Too many bystanders would be killed."

Nita looked around and saw that the policemen at the doors

were relaxing from tense poises. Their faces showed relief over Kirkpatrick's order.

An absolute hush lay upon the audience. The newspaper men sat rigidly, gripping the table, staring into the muzzle of a machine gun devoted entirely to them. The gangster who held it dropped down on the top step of the short flight from the stage. "You boys better sit quiet," he advised.

Nita was not thinking. She did not know what she had expected, but this was not it. Kirkpatrick sat down beside her, stolidly pulling up each trouser leg in turn to protect the crease. He gravely offered her a cigarette.

"Is…is this…?" Nita began.

"No," said Kirkpatrick quietly, "this is not part of the plan. Something has gone wrong."

Something! Everything had gone wrong. Nita fought down a mad impulse to burst into laughter. The despair she had struggled against throughout the day pushed up into her throat and strangled her. She did not realize that there was a renewed murmur of whispers all about her until, suddenly, that stopped. It was not a dying whisper such as the theater knows. It was instantaneous, breaths caught in the middle of a word. Her eyes flew to the platform.

From an ante-room of the stage, a swaggering broad-shouldered figure strode. He stalked to the front of the platform and stood in the center, looking out over the people. One of the machine gunners turned his head and looked at him, then faced front again. Three of the gangsters were seated, but their weapons were trained on the people before them. If one of them squeezed a trigger, a dozen persons would be blown into bloody death.

But all eyes were focused on the new arrival. He was not formally clad, but wore a black suit, shirt and tie. Over his face was a hood mask that was tucked neatly into a black collar. The face was formless beneath the hood. Eyes glittered from the slits.

The hush broke into a running murmur of sound: *"The Avenger!"*

A FEW men started to their feet, but subsided as the machine gunners tensed. A newspaper man tried to argue with the crook that held them prisoner and was almost slugged down with a black jack. Nita saw all these things subconsciously. Her eyes were fixed on the hooded man. He bowed suavely to the audience, then retired against the wall at the rear of the stage and stood on braced feet. His shoulders did not touch. There was about him an air of wary readiness.

"Damned clever," Kirkpatrick whispered in her ear, "if he really has kidnapped Dick."

Once more Nita felt the strange urge to laughter. Kirkpatrick could think of things like that when Dick might be dead! She touched her dress bag upon her knees, feeling the weight of the small automatic she carried there. She could kill the Avenger easily. It seemed unimportant that after she did that, she and a half-hundred others would be mowed down by fanning bullets.

She was aware that Kirkpatrick was still offering a cigarette. He leaned toward her, his eyes cool.

"No, Nita," he said. "Give Dick a chance."

Give Dick a chance? Didn't the fool know that he had no

chance? Even if he survived this ambuscade, the law would reach out a merciless hand. Nita felt her breath coming fast and sharply in her breast. Dick must come in his own identity, if at all, she realized sharply. Subconsciously, she had been looking for the bent and sinister figure in the cape, the Spider. But Dick could not come in that garb.

His mere appearance on the floor like that would be an instantaneous admission of all charges. Was Dick prepared to make even that sacrifice to rid the country of this menace which only the death of the leaders could wipe out? For the first time, she remembered Jackson's warning that the poison would next be distributed through candy bars. She turned and whispered that information to Kirkpatrick. He shook his head slightly.

"If Dick fails here tonight, we'll do our best to guard," he said, "but actually we are helpless. Our guard over medicine accomplished practically nothing. They must have another means of distribution. When I left headquarters, the reports were still coming in. Yesterday seven thousand died of poison over the country. Today, there were more than ten thousand more. Dick has taken the only way. God help him!"

Nita flung the cigarette to the floor. Her lower lip was caught in her teeth. Movement to her right jerked her head that way. Eddie Blanton was on his feet and sauntering toward the motionless Avenger. He ignored a machine gunner's angry order. Smoke streamed from his long cigarette holder. There was no tension in his movements, only languid disinterest. His shrewd long face looked sleepy.

The Avenger's head swung toward him and he gestured imperiously with his hand, ordering Blanton back. The newspaper man sauntered on and an automatic snapped into the hooded man's hand. Women gasped sharply, but Blanton kept on.

"It would be poor policy to shoot me here," he drawled, loudly enough for all to hear. "After all there are quite a number of rather reputable witnesses."

The Avenger appeared to hesitate, then shrugged and shoved the gun out of sight. Blanton stepped squarely in front of him, rested his elbows on the edge of the stage. The Avenger stepped forward and Blanton's voice dropped to inaudibles. The deep rumble of the Avenger's voice answered him, then Blanton swung about and strolled away.

"That isn't the Avenger," Nita said sharply to Kirkpatrick. "It is his helper, who goes in his clothing."

Kirkpatrick asked, "Why?"

"The Avenger would not have pulled a gun in the first place, any more than Dick would have," she said swiftly. "He would have known that Blanton couldn't be bluffed. And he would have realized that he couldn't do anything but bluff."

"I think you're right," said Kirkpatrick softly. "But I think that Dick has taken that into consideration, along with everything else." He drew a deep breath. "If only Dick is alive."

Abruptly the door by which the Avenger had entered swung open and a man stepped through and closed it behind him, stood with his twisted shoulders against it. The Avenger swung around, hand half-going to his gun, then he paused. The man in the doorway carried no weapon except a curved cane, on which he leaned.

Slowly, he shuffled forward, a long cape swinging from a hunched back, lank hair brushing out beneath a broad-brimmed, black hat. A beaked face peered upward from under it.

"My God!" A man's voice cracked thinly. "It's the Spider!"

CHAPTER 17
THE SPIDER DIES!

T HE SILENCE that dropped over the room was a shudder. People did not fear the Avenger. He was their Robin Hood, despite those four machine gunners who swung indolent legs from the edge of the stage. Those men were tense now. Two of them twisted their heads about on their shoulders to stare at the warped figure in the cloak that shambled toward the middle of the stage.

"Watch crowd," the Avenger's deep voice ordered and they turned stiffly back.

Nita had bowed her face into her hands and her shoulders shook with silent sobs. On, thank God! Thank God! Dick was alive. Alive, but... She jerked up her head, white-faced, eyes wide. He was alive, but why, why had he done this thing? Why had he come here in this disguise? It doomed him beyond any recall. It was a confession of guilt. It... Suddenly Nita *knew*. Dick had come here to die. He had come to kill his enemy and be killed. She sucked in a hissing breath and with it her shoulders straightened slowly. Her hand strayed again to the pearl-sewn bag upon her knee. Her fingers gripped it hard. But not alone! Dick should not die alone!

The twisted figure shambled on deliberately toward the Avenger, who faced him in a slight, tense crouch. The Spider made no gesture toward the audience. He seemed totally unaware of it—until Blanton got to his feet once more and sauntered forward.

The Spider's face swung toward him, expressionless, wooden. His voice reached everyone clearly, thickened by accent.

"Sit down, my child," he said calmly. "I feel that I am about to make a speech that will answer all your questions."

Nita caught a full view of his face for the first time and a small pucker tightened between her eyes. Then abruptly, she understood. Dick was wearing that steel mask he sometimes used when he had need to change identities quickly. That explained the immobility of his expression.

The Spider fluttered a hand indifferently in Blanton's direction and Blanton shrugged and with a smile he tried to make jeering, went back to his table. There was subdued laughter from the other newspaper men. It was all strangely out of place.

Nita's blood was thrumming through her ears. She could feel the slow, hard pumping of her heart. She was excited, but no longer frightened or worried. Dick was here now. That was all that mattered. He had come to die with his face to his enemies and she—she was ready, too. She held her breath as the Spider halted within ten feet of the Avenger and faced the audience.

"I must admit," he said in his thick, accented voice that was so different from his own clear tones, "to playing a trick upon my most efficient enemy, Commissioner Kirkpatrick. I promised him that if he would call this meeting tonight, I would appear and give my testimony. I intend to do that, but what I actually came for is to punish a treacherous fraud, the Avenger. When I have finished my little speech, I shall challenge the Avenger to duel. I do not think he will refuse."

He turned his head slowly toward the Avenger and the Hooded One was regarding him with a fixed, unswerving gaze.

"The Avenger has violated his agreement with me slightly," he said, waving an indifferent hand at the four machine gunners. "We were to meet on equal terms. Perhaps, he felt that this was making the arrangements quite equal, five to one."

The Spider laughed softly, mocking flat laughter that reached the farthest corners of the room, that made men shiver and women huddle their shoulders. Nita was listening with strained attention, a curious light in her eyes. Kirkpatrick's breath was audible to her. A fierce joy was pounding through her veins.

THE SPIDER was speaking again.

"I had suspected the Avenger of complicity in the poisonings that have killed some twenty-five thousand persons in the United States in the last ten days. Now I am sure. I need not go into my reasons, except to say that every move the Avenger has made has reinforced some detail of the poisoners' work.

"I tell you that this man, the Avenger, is guilty of twenty-five thousand murders and that he has pocketed millions as a result of those crimes!"

The Spider paused and there was not a sound in the audience. The machine gunners were hunched over their weapons. The Avenger moved a hand carelessly, as if he waved aside all these charges as so much air.

"This is ridiculous," he boomed. "People know how I serve them. Poisoner is man named Martin whom I soon turn over to police."

The Spider waited courteously until the other man had finished; then he spoke again, rapidly now, as if he were in a hurry to be done.

"This is not exactly the Avenger," the Spider asserted. "He is an underling called Ivan who sometimes performs work for the Avenger, and in that way establishes alibis. The real villain—" during a pause in which not a breath was heard, the Spider's eyes swept the audience. "The real villain is among you gentlemen out there." The sweep of his hand brought gasps of amazement, turned every man's suspicious eyes upon his neighbor.

"Presently" said the Spider harshly, "I shall name this villain for you. But first—" He whirled and wrenched at the cane. It became a glittering arc of steel, a saber. "First, I shall deal with the underling. *En garde,* Ivan! Draw your saber. You first; then your Master!"

A deep snarl came from the Hooded Man. From his trouser leg, he whisked out a blade and instantly they were upon each other, steel ringing and clanging. The Spider was crouched army style, clenched fist behind his back. The straight-up stance of the Avenger's man made him look ineffectual. Ivan was walking into the attack, his blade a whirling smother of metallic light. The saber was everywhere, smacking at head and shoulders, cutting at legs. And before the attack, the Spider retreated.

Nita sat tensely, hand gripping the automatic, her eyes following the swift give and take of the duel. She knew swordplay as only the Spider's mate could, and this....

Ivan's blade slithered past the Spider's guard and Nita gasped as the broad-brimmed hat was slashed from his head. The Spider crouched and his point jabbed home against the larger man's breast. Ivan reeled back under that blow and a harsh cry ripped from the Spider.

"A steel vest!" he cried. The Avenger's man wore armor! Nita felt a cold anger grow within her. She opened her bag slowly, gripped the automatic.

The Spider began a slashing attack that made the Russian's offensive seem a weak and futile thing. His blade was everywhere. Ivan stood up to it, abandoning all pretense of defense except that he protected his arms and legs. The steel vest made him impregnable to the assault. The Spider broke through and slashed to the head, and steel rang on steel.

Once more the Spider thrust with savage violence. The curved blade slithered out past the Russian's guard and once more grated on steel. But this time, from behind Ivan's hood came a muffled, fearful scream.

The Spider straightened, dropping the tip of his sword and Ivan staggered back. His arms flew high and his saber clattered to the floor. No more sound came from him; he smashed down on his back. Two of the machine gunners pivoted toward the two duelists.

The Spider ignored them. Red-tipped sword in hand, he sprang to the side of the fallen man, ripped off the hood. A steel casque like a ball covered the man's head. The Spider tugged that off also and showed the Russian's face, blood streaming from one eye. The Spider's point had gone through the eye-slit into his brain.

Nita felt exultation leap in her veins at the victory, but there was a fearful menace in those two machine guns. She eased over behind Kirkpatrick, her fingers groping in her bag again, closing fiercely about the butt of the automatic.

THE SPIDER held the steel casque high in his left hand and strode to the edge of the stage, still ignoring the machine gunners who pivoted with him, those dread muzzles gaping.

"This steel helmet," said the Spider, "proves what I have charged, that the Avenger and Martin, the head of the poison gang, are one and the same man. Martin never appeared before his gangsters unless his head was encased in this helmet. But this Ivan is not the man. He is an underling. The Master—"

Suddenly the Spider staggered. The steel casque dropped from his hand and hit the floor with a dull clangor. He caught at his throat, reeling. There was no sound at all then, except a woman's scream. Laughter lit the face of the machine gunner leaning against the arch. He thrust his body free and fondled his weapon.

"And that's that," he said calmly. "Everybody stand still, or—"

Nita was on her feet, the automatic clenched in her hand. The Spider was going backward, heavy-footed, and there was blood on his throat.

Suddenly the machine gunner stepped forward. "Drop those guns," he barked; then: *"Let them have it!"*

Two swift heavy shots put an exclamation point on his

sentence, and he rolled backward, dead on his feet. Nita jerked up her automatic and emptied it in a swift, light shatter of sound. She poured lead into the face of another of the machine gunners. The man reeled back a step, standing there dead; then blood began to seep from a half-dozen wounds in his face and forehead. He pitched forward across his weapon.

Nita looked down at the gun in her hand and shuddered, then glanced up with a feeling of unreality as a familiar voice cracked out, the voice of Richard Wentworth! She jerked her head about. The pale-faced croupier, Larue, was in the aisle with a heavy automatic in each fist, and the voice that came from his lips was the voice of Richard Wentworth!

"Get to Jackson, Kirk," Wentworth called sharply. "The man in the Spider outfit, Kirk. It's Jackson. I've got to get the Avenger!"

He plunged down the aisle, still gripping his guns, kicked aside a chair that skidded into his path. He hurled aside Commander Samuels who had scrambled out into the space before the stage. He did not halt until he reached the spot where the newspaper men crouched behind their table.

As he reached the table Blanton straightened from behind a chair, holding his long cigarette holder carelessly in his fingers. His long face was pale.

"Give your name to the press, me lad," he said jauntily. "We want to tell the people who saved the day for us all."

"Get your hands up, Blanton!" Wentworth snarled.

The reporter started, stared, and threw back his head and laughed. "Why, it's my old friend, Wentworth," he said. "I

181

thought for sure you were up there on the stage." He lifted the cigarette holder toward his lips.

"Get your hands up, I said," Wentworth snarled, and his two automatics centered on Blanton's chest. "You are the Avenger, the real Avenger, and you are Martin, too. When you shot the man you thought was the Spider, I saw that the bullet must have been fired from this side of the room. I could tell by the way your victim swayed, by the position of the wound. And then I knew.

"Nobody but a newspaper man would have known how to hound an enemy through the news as the Avenger did the Spider to keep him out of the way, while he cashed in on the poison plot. Nobody but you, Blanton, would have been smart enough to build the whole crazy plan. You had O'Burke and his lieutenant killed so you could take over his mob, and worked through it.

"I can prove that every time Martin or the real Avenger has appeared, you've been on the scene. You were a friend of Mannley's and many other crooks and you knew how to handle them. But it was your job to know them, so you escaped suspicion."

BLANTON WAS fumbling with the cigarette holder and the grin was still on his horsey face. "Scarcely legal evidence, my dear Wentworth," he sneered.

"Quite right, Blanton," he said, "and you had me fooled for a while. I couldn't understand that play of hostility between the Avenger and Martin, but I gather now that you wanted me to carry word of that fact to Kirkpatrick. You were so confident of killing me that you even had Patsy Malone phone Jackson to come and free me. The fact that four of your men were killed made no difference to you so long as you got word to authorities of hostility between Martin and the Avenger. After I was dead, that would totally confuse them and you would have no trouble in arranging your getaway.

"You intended at this show tonight for Ivan to be killed, then for your machine gunners to kill the Spider. When police killed your machine gunners, there would be no member of the gang left. Martin and the Avenger could both disappear and the crime would be unsolved, while you pocketed your millions."

Blanton's grin was mocking now. "Is this all the evidence against me?" he queried. "It sounds like balderdash to me."

Wentworth shook his head. "No, but there are two other little matters that will convict you. First of all, Martin had weak ankles. It was clear from the way he ran and the fact that he wore high boots. You wear high-topped shoes yourself and have weak ankles. You're knock-kneed as hell. And you still have on your person the gun with which you shot Jackson as he was about to denounce you, as you thought."

The newspaper men were straightening from their frightened positions, staring with amazed eyes from Blanton, who was their idol, to this pale-faced man whom Blanton addressed as Wentworth, but who looked nothing on earth like that man. Blanton turned to his friends with a shrug.

"Did any of you see or hear me shoot?" he asked with a quizzical smile.

"A silencer," Wentworth interrupted.

"A silencer?" Blanton jerked. "They won't work on either revolvers or automatics, and you know it. The gases are kicked back and blast out through the back of an automatic or cut the side of a revolver and make almost as much noise as if the silencer weren't on them. Only a few fool fiction writers think silencers will work on hand arms."

"Give me your cigarette holder!" Wentworth snapped.

He lunged toward Blanton, but he was too late. He felt a numbing shock in his side that made him sway and knew he'd been shot. He saw Blanton drop the cigarette holder and snatch an automatic from beneath his arm, then both Wentworth's guns spoke together.

"Good God, Wentworth, you've killed him!"

Lanky Gallahan was pillowing Blanton's head in his arms. "You're crazy, Wentworth, crazy!" he gabbled.

Blanton's head rolled, his eyes opened slowly. Miraculously, the man was still alive despite two big-caliber bullets through his vitals.

"Not crazy, Gallahan," Blanton mumbled. "Damn... smart!" He closed his eyes, his chest heaving spasmodically. "Gang way... palsy. I'll mess up... your...!"

He wrenched. A torrent of blood poured from his mouth. He shuddered and lay still. Wentworth stooped heavily, and picked up the cigarette holder. It was much thicker than the one Blanton ordinarily used and no tobacco smoke ever had dribbled through it. He wrenched it open and revealed a single-shot pistol arrangement with a silencer on its muzzle.

"An automatic or a revolver can't use a silencer," Wentworth said slowly, "but a single shot weapon has no opening for the noisy gases to pop out of. It makes no sound at all. That's how he shot Jackson—and me!"

JACKSON! THE word sounded an alarm in Wentworth's mind. Jackson was wounded, perhaps dying because he had fought for Wentworth, taken the Spider's place, taken the bullet intended for the Spider. Wentworth turned heavily toward the stairs and the stage where Jackson stood with his shoulders braced against the wall. He had a gun in his hand and he was holding off Nita and Kirkpatrick and a half-dozen other men.

"… This is the truth," Jackson was saying clearly. "I used Wentworth's home as a base of operations. I used the cover of his name. That is why he has so often been blamed. But I, and I alone, am the Spider!"

A woman went past Wentworth, shouldered through the crowd. "He's lying," she snapped. "He's not…."

Wentworth saw that the woman was Patsy Malone, he saw Jackson's gun coming up and shouted a hoarse warning. The gun convulsed and barked from Jackson's hand. Patsy's voice rose in a piercing cry and her small body slammed back against a man behind her. Even as his arms flew out to catch her, she slumped to the floor. She was dead before she hit.

Wentworth saw a man whip out a revolver and level it at Jackson, but he reached the wrist in time and put all his weight on it.

"Don't," he said hoarsely. "Don't! She had it coming to her." He slumped down on his knees, facing Jackson.

"The dirty… little tramp," said Jackson. "She tricked me from the start…!"

185

Wentworth reached out his hand and pulled off the Spider mask. Jackson was grinning weakly.

"Howdy… Major," he gasped. "I guess it's… taps this time… all right."

Wentworth felt something hard as stone in his throat. He was pressing the palm of his left hand against the wound in his side, staying the hemorrhage.

"Jackson, you damned fool" he said slowly. "All those lies." He worked a little closer on his knees. "Come on, Jack, we got to get you to the hospital."

Jackson shook his head wearily. It rolled on the wall. "No go, Major. I got it," he gasped. "But, say, is… everything all right? I kind of messed… you up."

Through his own swelling pain, Wentworth felt a stinging in his eyes. He had been a fool ever to doubt Jackson, but the weight of the evidence had been so strongly against him. He seemed to have gone haywire over that girl. And Jackson had made amends.

"Everything's swell, Jack," he said. "But, damn your soul, why did you do it? You're a hell of a swell soldier and nothing could ever make it different. You're loyal, square…."

"Save the bouquets, Major," Jackson's breath was coming in short gasps now. "I'll… need them later."

Wentworth heard a woman's sob and was aware that Nita was on her knees beside him.

"Good-bye, Miss." Jackson writhed. "Good… bye… Major."

The life went out of his body in a breath. Wentworth felt as if his own life was gone, too. He lifted his head slowly. "A good soldier," he said heavily, "but an awful liar. Everybody knows he wasn't the Spider. It's... silly...."

Wentworth did not see Kirkpatrick's hand grasping a gun, did not see Kirkpatrick, stooping forward as if to help him, slap that gun heavily behind his ear. He felt a blaze of light. Then soft black darkness and dived into unconsciousness. Kirkpatrick straightened. "Get this man to a hospital, quickly," he snapped. "He's wounded!"

CHAPTER 18
LONG LIVE THE SPIDER!

WHEN WENTWORTH regained consciousness, he was in the hospital with Kirkpatrick and Nita beside him. He found that his voice was weak and that intolerable pain throbbed through his side. He twisted toward Kirkpatrick.

"Kirk," he said weakly. "You didn't let Jackson take the rap like that, did you? The fool was lying, lying to make up to me for his blunders."

Kirkpatrick smiled thinly. "You've been pretty sick, Dick," he said. "You'll be glad to know we wiped out the last of the O'Burke-Martin gang. You killed the Avenger and Martin in one man. We found both disguises hidden among the toys of Blanton's kid."

Wentworth tossed his head fretfully. "Listen," he said, "You're stalling. I won't let Jackson be buried with a blot on his name. He never was against me. He just blundered in trusting that girl. When he kidnapped me from your office, I didn't know. He took me to a rooming house and tied me up tight. I told him that he was jeopardizing my entire plan, that he had made me break my word by kidnapping me. Being a prisoner forced me to tell my plans and Jackson said he'd take my place. He executed all my plans marvelously. He got that Spider kit somewhere, God only knows where, and used the saber as I had taught him to do."

Wentworth stopped, closed his eyes, fought them open again. "I finally got free of Jackson's ropes, disguised myself as the croupier, Larue, and made my way to the hall. It had been my intention to force the Avenger and Martin to kill me, thus convicting themselves. They would then have been executed and I would have escaped the humiliation and pain of the courts.

"When I found it was impossible to locate and stop Jackson, I decided to carry on with the same idea in a different way. I would sit on the sidelines and block any attempts to hurt Jackson. I watched the suspects, Commander Samuels and Marshant. I'll admit Blanton eluded my suspicions, until I saw that the shot that killed Jackson must have been fired from the news table. Then I knew."

Wentworth was very tired. "Listen, Kirk," he said. "I want Jackson cleared."

Kirkpatrick interrupted roughly. "Don't be a fool, Dick. Jackson is the most honored soldier who ever went to his grave. The entire city turned out for his funeral. Newspapers are singing paeans to his glory, recalling all the services the Spider rendered to mankind. Soldiers marched behind his coffin and the President himself ordered that he be buried in Arlington."

"That'll help a lot now that he's dead," Wentworth said bitterly.

Kirkpatrick leaned forward. "What I am pointing out to you," he said shortly, "is that there is no sense in your making a foolish sacrifice of yourself. Jackson took the blame and the glory with him.

"Incidentally, he made it impossible for you to be convicted. He explained every bit of evidence that we have against you. He stole the automatic that killed Mannley, wore your signet ring on his finger, so the motion picture the Avenger took is useless. Another motion picture that was taken out in Chicago showed Jackson fighting the Avenger, but the latter half of it was too dim to be properly developed. The Avenger said it showed you, but we couldn't find you. The Avenger said he had another bit of evidence that went to smash, literally, a picture of you and Nita escaping police from your apartment, a thing for which Jackson takes blame. But that plate was broken when the Avenger took it from the newspaper photographer who snapped it.

"If you insist on making a confession, the courts will have to consider it, of course, but I doubt that you could convict yourself even if you tried after that grandstand finish in which Jackson killed the Avenger's man. Personally, I believe you're out of your head with fever." He smiled slightly, parting his mustache with thumb and forefinger.

"And by the way, don't feel too bad about Jackson and Patsy Malone. He didn't kill her exclusively because of her betrayals of you. She was the wife of that man, Coxwell, who brought their baby to the meeting. She fooled Jackson the whole time."

189

Wentworth's hand was upon Nita's now. There was a great pain within him at the loss of Jackson, but there was a great peace, too. Jackson had been loyal to his salt. He smiled wanly at Nita.

"It seems," he said slowly, "that the Spider is dead."

"Let him stay dead," Kirkpatrick urged.

Wentworth turned his face toward him. "I suspect that a Spider must always rise to help the people when they need a champion. As long as the nation is held in the thrall of criminal madmen, there must be a Spider to fight them. One Spider is dead. A more gallant man never lived."

"The Spider is dead!" Nita said, and there was a sob in her throat. It was both sorrow for Jackson and for the happiness she had dreamed of that now was fading. For Wentworth had been washed clean of crimes by Jackson's blood sacrifice. The book was wiped clean of charges against him. For the brief hours that had passed between Jackson's death and now, she had nourished a little, secret dream that she knew in her heart was false. She had known, actually, that Wentworth would never cease his crusades of justice while life was in his body, but the dream that they might go away together had been so sweet... Her hands tightened upon Wentworth's, and the sob welled up once more and died. She was proud of this warrior man of hers. She would not have him otherwise. Her head came up.

"The Spider is dead," she said, with a breathless little laugh. *"Long Live the Spider!"*

POPULAR HERO PULPS AVAILABLE NOW:

THE SPIDER

☐ #1: The Spider Strikes — $13.95
☐ #2: The Wheel of Death — $13.95
☐ #3: Wings of the Black Death — $13.95
☐ #4: City of Flaming Shadows — $13.95
☐ #5: Empire of Doom! — $13.95
☐ #6: Citadel of Hell — $13.95
☐ #7: The Serpent of Destruction — $13.95
☐ #8: The Mad Horde — $13.95
☐ #9: Satan's Death Blast — $13.95
☐ #10: The Corpse Cargo — $13.95
☐ #11: Prince of the Red Looters — $13.95
☐ #12: Reign of the Silver Terror — $13.95
☐ #13: Builders of the Dark Empire — $13.95
☐ #14: Death's Crimson Juggernaut — $13.95
☐ #15: The Red Death Rain — $13.95
☐ #16: The City Destroyer — $13.95
☐ *NEW:* #17: The Pain Emperor — $13.95

OPERATOR 5

☐ #1: The Masked Invasion — $13.95
☐ #2: The Invisible Empire — $13.95
☐ #3: The Yellow Scourge — $13.95
☐ #4: The Melting Death — $13.95
☐ #5: Cavern of the Damned — $13.95
☐ #6: Master of Broken Men — $13.95
☐ #7: Invasion of the Dark Legions — $13.95
☐ #8: The Green Death Mists — $13.95
☐ *NEW:* #9: Legions of Starvation — $13.95

THE MYSTERIOUS WU FANG

☐ #1: The Case of the Six Coffins — $12.95
☐ #2: The Case of the Scarlet Feather — $12.95
☐ #3: The Case of the Yellow Mask — $12.95
☐ #4: The Case of the Suicide Tomb — $12.95
☐ #5: The Case of the Green Death — $12.95
☐ #6: The Case of the Black Lotus — $12.95
☐ #7: The Case of the Hidden Scourge — $12.95

G-8 AND HIS BATTLE ACES

☐ #1: The Bat Staffel — $13.95

CAPTAIN SATAN

☐ #1: The Mask of the Damned — $13.95
☐ #2: Parole for the Dead — $13.95
☐ #3: The Dead Man Express — $13.95
☐ #4: A Ghost Rides the Dawn — $13.95
☐ #5: The Ambassador From Hell — $13.95

DUSTY AYRES AND HIS BATTLE BIRDS

☐ #1: Black Lightning! — $13.95
☐ #2: Crimson Doom — $13.95
☐ #3: The Purple Tornado — $13.95
☐ #4: The Screaming Eye — $13.95
☐ #5: The Green Thunderbolt — $13.95
☐ #6: The Red Destroyer — $13.95
☐ #7: The White Death — $13.95
☐ #8: The Black Avenger — $13.95
☐ #9: The Silver Typhoon — $13.95
☐ #10: The Troposphere F-S — $13.95
☐ #11: The Blue Cyclone — $13.95
☐ #12: The Tesla Raiders — $13.95

DR. YEN SIN

☐ #1: Mystery of the Dragon's Shadow — $12.95
☐ #2: Mystery of the Golden Skull — $12.95
☐ #3: Mystery of the Singing Mummies — $12.95

MAVERICKS

☐ #1: Five Against the Law — $12.95
☐ #2: Mesquite Manhunters — $12.95
☐ #3: Bait for the Lobo Pack — $12.95
☐ #4: Doc Grimson's Outlaw Posse — $12.95
☐ #5: Charlie Parr's Gunsmoke Cure — $12.95